PENNIES FROM HEAVEN

PENNIES FROM HEAVEN

Prairie Stories from
the Great Depression

Ralph Schmidt

ISBN: 1-55430-021-5
BookSurge Publishing Canada
905 Fort Street, Victoria, BC Canada V8V 3K3

If you enjoyed reading my stories, please send me a line. If you have a good story from the Great Depression era - let's see it. Maybe I'll come up with another book.

Mr. Ralph Schmidt
979 Ridgeway Street
Victoria, BC Canada
V8X 3C2
(250) 727-2810

ACKNOWLEDGEMENTS

So many people have helped me complete this book.

First, I should acknowledge my family. My gratitude to my wife Jane, for her encouragement and her forbearance in allowing me to occasionally clutter up the dining room table with partially written stories. Thanks also to my sister Lucille Hunter and my cousin Verla Koob for delving into the past and helping me to unravel some of these old stories. My gratitude also goes out to my niece Julie Mendgen for her many constructive editorial comments.

The illustrations express the combined efforts of several artists. My son Paul prepared preliminary sketches. The finishing work was done by Elayne Erickson, Bill Leach, Paul Nysted and Peggy Fawcett. To all of them, I take off my hat and bow appreciatively.

My thanks are also due to Mary Pankowski, my creative writing teacher, who tactfully inspired me to try again and again to turn out a good story.

My thanks also to my neighbour Kathleen Burgess for her editing work.

And finally, my gratitude to Elayne Erickson who not only did my typing, but also made many constructive suggestions on all aspects of my story telling. Without her help in keeping me on track, I would never have made it.

CONTENTS

PREFACE

The survivors of the Great Depression are gradually disappearing. The thinning of their ranks closely parallels that of World War II veterans who somehow managed to survive both the Depression and the war.

My stories originate from these survivors. I am very grateful to each one who shared a memory with me, and I would like to dedicate my book to them. During the time it has taken to write this book, four of them have already died. For those few, this dedication can only be addressed to my memory of them.

I am happy to have the opportunity to preserve their stories for the rest of us to enjoy.

CANADA
N
ALBERTA
LEGEND / LÉGENDE
International boundary / Frontière internationale
Provincial boundary / Limite provinciale
Scale / Échelle
75 0 75 150 225
km km

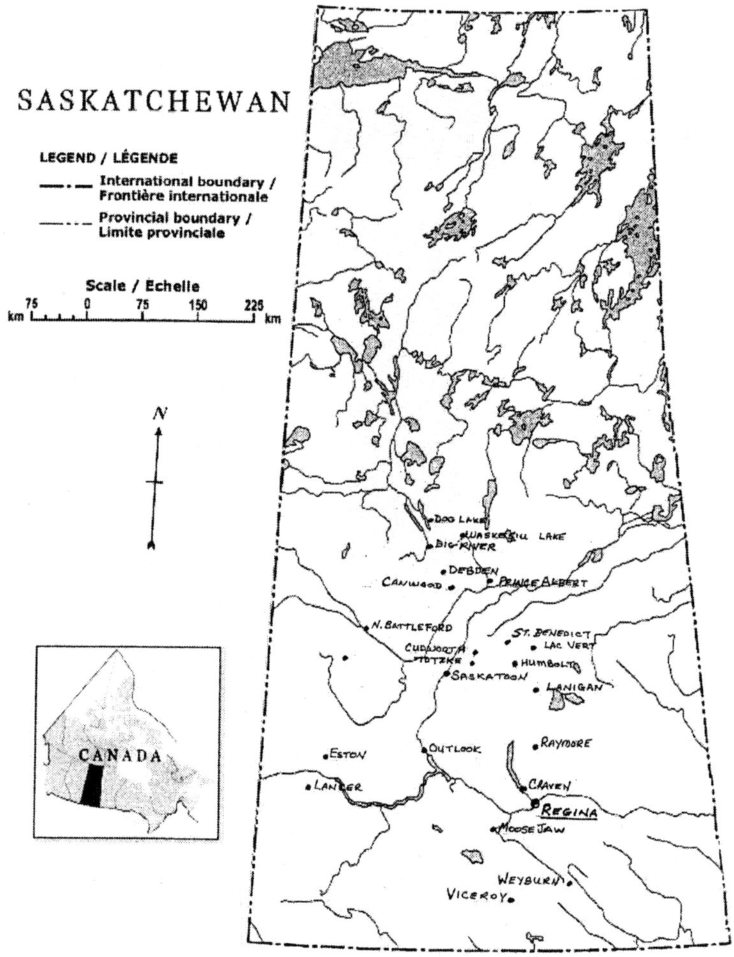
SASKATCHEWAN
LEGEND / LÉGENDE
International boundary / Frontière internationale
Provincial boundary / Limite provinciale
Scale / Échelle
75 0 75 150 225
km km
N
CANADA
BIG RIVER
DEBDEN
CANWOOD
PRINCE ALBERT
N. BATTLEFORD
ST. BENEDICT
LAC VERT
HUMBOLDT
SASKATOON
LANIGAN
RAYMORE
ESTON
OUTLOOK
CRAVEN
REGINA
MOOSE JAW
WEYBURN
VICEROY

Part I

SUMMER HOLIDAYS

Summer holidays, for most school kids during the Depression, did not have the same appeal as they do today. There were fewer "toys", fewer diversions, and fewer opportunities to indulge in activities which cost money. The biggest, single enjoyment that summer holidays offered was the mere fact that for a couple of months we were free from school. Free from the discipline. Free from the homework.

Families who were not well-off did not have the means to indulge in camping trips, or in renting a cottage by a lake, or in traveling to distant places. My father owned a 1929 Chevrolet sedan. During the Depression he could not afford to operate this car. It was stored on blocks in our garage. During the winter we used it as a deep freeze, storing various cuts of meat, plus fifty pounds of white fish.

I don't suppose that this car had traveled more than a couple thousand miles when my dad sold it in 1938 to pay for my oldest sister's education.

In 1929, our family enjoyed a camping holiday (see "My Earliest Childhood Memories"). At the time, we did not realize that this event would be the first, the last , and the only time that our family would ever have a summer holiday together. The Depression took care of that.

My greatest enjoyment during the summer holidays centred around activities with friends and relatives who were near my age. We often enjoyed playing traditional games that our older siblings had taught us, such as hide-and-seek or run-sheep-run. But we also made good use of our imaginations and discovered different ways of passing the time and having fun (see "Show Biz").

Pennies from Heaven

When I was growing up in small-town Saskatchewan, there was always a shortage of pocket money in our family. While my father's earnings provided us with the essentials of life, they didn't extend to some of the frills which our well-to-do neighbours took for granted.

I became accustomed to "tough times" at a young and tender age. It was necessary to become self-reliant and devise ways and means of generating my own "cash flow". Perhaps I should say "penny trickle", because even the most successful business venture during my boyhood never did produce much money. Usually just a penny here and a penny there, just enough to buy a handful of licorice or a dozen jaw breakers at the drugstore.

Collecting and selling empty beer bottles proved to be my most continuous and sustained source of petty cash after I passed my twelfth birthday. There was considerable competition from classmates to pick up these bottles, so I used to start my search at 5:00 AM. I called it the dawn patrol. I would set out optimistically with a gunny sack over my shoulder.

After a dance night in the Cudworth town hall, I would scout the areas where young couples would usually park a car in some degree of privacy. These necking spots or "passion pits" usually yielded several abandoned empty beer bottles which had contributed to the evening's enjoyment.

Another penny-producing enterprise at that time was the collection and sale of Libby labels, mostly from tin cans. The Libby food company offered boy scout equipment, badges and clothing in exchange for labels from their products. I don't recall the exact figures, but it took hundreds of Libby labels to acquire a boy scout knife. Libby's pork and beans cans were my primary source of labels. They were very cheap, nutritious, and could be enjoyed unheated eaten out of the can; a very popular meal during the lean years of the depression.

A local grocer's teenaged son was an aspiring boy scout. He paid one cent for four Libby labels. I collected these labels wherever I could, even making "scouting " trips to the town dump, where I foraged through piles of tin cans.

Yes, we had to be innovative and energetic in order to earn small change. Perhaps the most unusual money-making scheme that I ever undertook involved the location and extraction of coins from beneath Cudworth sidewalks.

Until after World War II, Cudworth had no paved streets whatsoever and, of course, no concrete sidewalks. During the pioneer days of this little town, the main street and a few others had been surfaced with a shallow layer of gravel. Most of the streets were just unimproved dirt roads liberally decorated with horse droppings. In wet weather, depressions in the road became slippery, muddy and deeply rutted. In dry weather they became very dusty. Occasionally little dust devils would twirl and dance down the streets.

Very few sidewalks graced the streets of Cudworth. The very longest stretch of boardwalk extended for five blocks along Main street, from St. Michael's Roman Catholic Church to the drugstore where the street came to an abrupt halt across from the CN station. The surface of these boardwalks consisted of two-by-six boards nailed to a couple of stringers on the ground. The boards were spaced about three-quarters of an inch apart. Few people realized just how important this small space was.

One day my friend Raymond Spainy and I were returning to his home after selling a few pop bottles we had found by the railroad track. Raymond accidentally dropped a penny on the sidewalk. It was one of those huge pennies that were minted until the early twenties. When it fell, the penny immediately disappeared into one of the sidewalk spaces.

We dropped to our hands and knees and began to search. In less than a minute we discovered his penny; but more importantly, we detected another one just a few inches away. Perhaps this sidewalk would present a new economic opportunity. We continued our search and we were successful in finding several more coins. We used a pocket knife to mark a small X on the sidewalk at each site of discovery. We then started to devise a method of retrieving the coins from beneath the sidewalk.

Using two long slender splints of wood in a chopstick fashion, we were able to lift a penny, but we couldn't hold it between the splints long enough to bring it to the surface. After becoming completely frustrated, we went to Raymond's home and selected a hammer and a goose neck pry bar from his father's tool box. Although we were only nine years old, it took us only a few minutes to pry the board loose and pull up the nails on one end. We were then able to lever the board high enough to reach underneath and grab the coins. We carefully re-nailed the board in place and decided to continue with this sidewalk venture. Over the next couple of days we managed to find nearly twenty cents. But then we became a little careless in replacing the sidewalk boards in our haste to get on to the next discovery. This matter was pointedly drawn to our attention by members of the business community, including my dad, and we were forbidden to continue with our project.

I don't know whether any other enterprising lads emulated our venture in later years; I feel certain that there is still a four and a half block trail of pennies, now covered by modern concrete sidewalks.

During the summer holidays we would sometimes hang around the "down town" area on days when a big soft drink truck from Saskatoon would make deliveries to the drug store and the cafes. The truck driver always seemed to be in a rush, and would welcome the services of a couple of strong boys to help him carry the crates of pop from the truck into a place of business. A couple of us would help him out, after which we then enjoyed a free tepid bottle of Orange Crush or Pepsi Cola as the truck disappeared in a cloud of dust down the highway to the next town.

I also tried my hand at earning money in mid-summer as a door-to-door salesman. I peddled big, luscious saskatoon berries. Without a doubt these berries were the most flavourful of all berries known to man. One would think that they would be in high demand. The demand may well have been there, but in most depression households, the money was not available.

After picking a five-pound lard pail of saskatoons, I would select the biggest most luscious berries, and place them in full view at the top, and knock on doors asking twenty-five cents for a full pail.

Sometimes I was successful, sometimes not. It did not distress me if I could not sell them, because my mom would bake a pie. Everyone knows that a saskatoon berry pie is the most tasty pie in the world, with or without soft ice-cream.

Just after the onset of World War II, when I was fifteen years old, another money-making opportunity emerged. Apparently the Canadian war industries were facing shortages in strategic war materials. As a consequence, the Canadian government promoted a salvage and recycling program. The word went out that the government would buy scrap metal and bones. Apparently the bones were used in the manufacture of explosives.

One of the grain elevator agents was assigned the task of buying these materials and eventually shipping them by rail to eastern Canada where the war industries were located.

When my friend Ray Wunderlich and I first heard of this opportunity we immediately sprang to action. We focused our attention on pasture lands. We walked through hundreds of acres east of Cudworth, picking up cow bones and horse bones and stuffing them into gunny sacks. When a sack was full we hid it in the bush until such time as we could pick it up in a vehicle.

After completing the collection stage of this venture, we "borrowed" a 1927 Chevrolet sedan belonging to Ray's dad, first removing the back seat in order to accommodate the maximum load of bones.

One day right after supper, we drove into the country to retrieve the bones that we had collected. It was early summer, and the ground had not yet firmed up in all places. As we drove across-country through pasture land, we realized that we must drive carefully to avoid soft spots.

We collected all of the gunny sacks packed with bones and piled them in the back seat of the car until it was filled up to the roof. Daylight was fading rapidly as we headed across the pasture to the main road. We were feeling very satisfied with our 'bones' operation when disaster struck. Our load of bones was very heavy and when the rear wheels hit a soft spot in the pasture we were stuck. The wheels spun until they sank right up to the axle. Although we were less than a hundred feet from the road, it may as well have been a hundred miles.

We would not be able to move the car unless we got help. It was getting dark. We would have to take action real soon.

The nearest farm house was about a quarter mile away. We knew the farmer well. He played saxophone in a band that played for our hockey dances. Maybe he would help us out. We jogged to his house. To our dismay the house was in total darkness.

We hesitated momentarily at the door, but realizing that this was the only help available, we began knocking on the door, at first very tentatively, but when we got no response we began pounding. Eventually a light went on, and we were soon excitedly explaining our predicament. The farmer was very friendly. He harnessed a team of horses and we trudged across the field to the car. There was a sliver of a moon so we were not in total darkness.

In a matter of minutes we were again mobile. We thanked the farmer profusely. He did not expect any money for his help and, of course, we had none to give.

I don't remember the exact amount of money that we were paid for the bones, but I recall that we each bought a ten cent pack of Sweet Caporal cigarettes and still had more than a dollar left over.

Next day at school we were boastfully telling two of our classmates about our successful undertaking. After we finished our explanation, they glanced at each other and almost collapsed with laughter. We were puzzled at their response. What the heck was going on?

One of the boys explained: "Look here, you guys. You earned some good money, but you've gone about it the wrong way entirely. Too much energy expended for so small a reward."

Now we really were puzzled. "Come on, explain yourself."

Mike replied, barely able to keep a straight face, "My buddy and I are also in the bone salvage business, but we developed our own system, much more efficient than yours. In the middle of the night we sneak down to the grain elevator and fill up our gunny sacks from that huge pile of bones waiting for shipment. The next day we sell them back. It's what you might call a double recycling operation."

Ray and I were astounded and we thought that we just might try this method ourselves. Certainly there would be no danger of getting stuck in the mud.

Meanwhile, the town council hired a watchman to guard the bones. During his first night on the job he caught our two smart-aleck classmates. Ray and I snuffed out our bone recycling venture. Our next contribution to the war effort was joining the RCAF.

More Pennies from Heaven

The stories presented in "Pennies from Heaven" describe the activities of a boy hoping to earn a little money in a very small Saskatchewan community.

As one would expect, a boy growing up in the city during the Depression faced a much different set of circumstances.

My friend Bob was raised in the city of Saskatoon where the amenities of the modern world far exceeded anything that my little village had to offer.

To a young lad, one of the greatest disparities between village and city life was the quality of entertainment. In Cudworth, we had no theatre. Periodically, (at best, bi-weekly) a travelling projectionist would show a movie in the town hall. Viewing a movie was often obstructed because the floor was not sloping. The only seating available were uncomfortable benches with no back support. Sore backs were common after show time.

Here are some of Bob's memories about seeing movies in Saskatoon during the Depression.

* * *

Our favourite movie house was the Roxy. Every Saturday morning, it was filled with rowdy, noisy kids, long before the matinee began.

Our second choice was the Tivoli. In order to attract a full house, this theatre would occasionally feature a real-live cowboy on the stage before the main show started. We cheered and hollered and blew spit-balls with enthusiasm as the cowboy did his best to entertain us. He usually tried to scare us by performing sudden menacing moves with his toy gun, or by varying the volumc of his voice from a whisper to a loud roar. His best act was a terrible tumble from an imaginary bronco. By the time he was finished with his routine, we were in the mood for an exciting cowboy show.

Of course, if you were going to see a movie, you had to have some money. Allowances did not exist in most families, so we used our ingenuity to get into the movies.

We discovered that we could earn money by catching fish and selling them to the workers in the Chinese laundry.

The city had constructed a low dam across the South Saskatchewan River to increase water storage capacity. Near the shore, a gently graded channel had been constructed to provide the fish with easy access over the dam. For safety reasons, this fish ladder and dam were out of bounds to everyone. A fence had been built to keep the public off the site. Periodically, the area was patrolled by "old man Ward", an elderly policeman pedaling a bike.

It took three of us to conduct this poaching operation. One boy took up a position as a lookout on the public walkway in case the policeman came by. The second boy stood on the outside of the fence, while the third boy (usually me, because I was tall for my age) would vault the fence, catch the fish and toss them over the fence to the boy outside of it.

It was not difficult to catch the carp as they sluggishly swam up the shallow channel. I would position my right hand in the opaque water until I felt a good-sized fish. To catch it, I would pounce on it with both hands and try to pin it against the bottom of the concrete channel. Then I would grasp it firmly below the gills and fling it to my buddy on the other side of the fence.

After catching several fish, we would visit the Chinese laundry and sell our catch for five cents a piece.

During periods when the fish were not moving in the channel, we sought other means of getting to see a movie. I remember going to a movie with a neighbour boy whose nickname was Baby, because he always seemed to be sniffling. I had five cents in my pocket. When I asked him if he had any money, he shrugged and muttered crossly, "Don't worry, I'll get in."

Upon arriving at the Tivoli, I paid for my admission. Suddenly, Baby crouched down near the door and began to weep plaintively. The girl selling tickets became disturbed. "What's the matter with him?"

I replied, "He has no money to get in."

She hesitated for a moment, then leaned over and whispered, "Here's a ticket for him. It's on the house."

He may have been called Baby, but in my opinion, he sure knew how to operate..

Sometimes, the rear entrance of the Capital would be used to admit customers (in addition to the main entrance). At the rear, there was a very small lobby separated from the main seating area by heavy black drapes.

One day when my buddy and I were broke, we waited until the ticket seller's view was obstructed by a big customer. Using this cover, we scampered behind the drapes. Our dog, a gentle black cocker spaniel, moved invisibly with us and soon made itself comfortable on a seat where it curled up and went to sleep.

Some time later, a dog in the movie kicked up a fuss. It was chasing a squirrel and began barking furiously. The noise woke up our dog, who immediately began to bark much louder than the dog in the movie.

A teen-aged usherette heard our dog barking as well as the accompanying hoots and howls of the kids sitting nearby. She hurried down the aisle, probing along the rows of seats with a flashlight. By the time she reached our section, the dog in the movie had stopped barking, and our cocker spaniel had resumed his slumber. She spied our dog, but decided against taking action.

In order to present a more enticing attraction for pre-teenagers, the theatres would often show a serial movie, with a new episode each week for a total of twelve weeks. I still have memories of Buck Jones, Tom Mix, and Rin Tin Tin.

Prizes were another attraction. I won a toque for guessing the correct number of puffed wheat kernels in a large glass jar. By far, the biggest winner was Tommy Jakes (three or four years older than me) who won a real live Shetland pony. This little horse soon adopted his new owner and treated him gently. But it would never allow anyone else on its back, not even the school bully.

Some of the theatres had a fire exit on the second floor. One Saturday evening, our little group was flat broke. We first tried to gain entry through a side door. We were unsuccessful. Then we climbed a ladder leading to a fire escape. Sometimes, the fire escape exit would be purposely left ajar to provide a little fresh air. Not so today! The door was locked. We were stymied. In our frustration, we sat down on the platform and took in the view. We looked across the alley into several lit-up hotel rooms. One room was occupied by a woman in bed. Right next to her, an almost bald head poked up from the covers. At first, we thought it belonged to a baby, but it turned out to be a very small man who was completely bald.

Things soon began to happen on that bed. The entertainment provided to us, while free, could well have been classified "for adults only".

We enjoyed a broad range of entertainment in those days, when even small change was difficult to acquire.

My Earliest Childhood Memories

My early childhood memories do not reach as far back into the past as those of some people I have met over the years.

I'm certainly not in the same category as a friend of mine, who swears he can still recall an event that took place several times during the first year of his life. He remembers competing with his twin brother for the most productive nipple during breast feeding time. During my seventy-nine years on this earth, I have met no one who could match that feat of memory. My very earliest memories stem from boyhood experiences during the summer of 1929, when I was four years old. Economic conditions were favourable, and our family could easily afford a camping holiday at Lake Waskesiu in Prince Albert National Park.

I remember an event that occurred during a fishing trip on Lake Waskesiu. There were three of us in a row boat: my father, my grandfather and me. It was a warm sunny morning. Not a breath of wind ruffled the water's surface. The day was quiet and relaxing. The only sounds were the muffled knockings from the oarlocks and from the swirling water as my father slowly rowed the boat. The warmth and the dreamy monotony made me drowsy, so I curled up on some jackets in the bow of the boat and drifted off to sleep.

Some time later, my slumber was gently disturbed by my grandfather. I gradually became aware that he was softly patting my cheek, and whispering excitedly.

"Ralph, wake up, wake up! I want you to see something very special."

I was in a deep sleep, and I responded very slowly. When I did open my eyes, Grampa shook my shoulder vigorously and whispered, "Look over there toward the shore."

My eyes followed his pointing finger and I saw the huge animal. At that moment the gigantic bull moose was raising its massive head from the water. There was green stuff hanging from its mouth, and several streams of water dripping from its long dewlap.

We were then so close to the shore that I could clearly see his eyes. I was sure that he was glaring at me. I got scared, but not for long. He lifted his nose a few inches, grunted a couple of times and slowly turned to leave the lake. He soon disappeared in the jack pine forest. Then I noticed that my fingers hurt. I had been fiercely clenching my fists during the entire event.

* * *

My next memory episode also occurred during this camping vacation. I was again awakened from a deep sleep. This time it occurred in the middle of the night, and it was not an enjoyable experience.

I guess that it was the noise that woke me up. Inside the tent my mother and father were yelling instructions and my two older sisters were screaming as they all desperately clutched the bottom of the tent along the side facing the lake. Outside the tent the booming sound of thunder combined with a howling wind provided a fearsome background. Suddenly, there was a horrible tearing sound as a tree was uprooted and smashed to the ground just a few feet from the tent. This was just too much for me. I covered my head with a blanket and cried.

The tent withstood the storm, and never did collapse or get blown away, but it took ages for the wind to finally settle down. Then we discovered that most of the bedding was wet. Oh, the joys of camping!

The next day the park warden told my dad that several tents had been torn apart by the storm. According to my dad, our tent held together because my mother had made it. She used very heavy-weight canvas and the seams were double sewn on her treadle Singer sewing machine.

* * *

On this same camping vacation, I remember being awakened yet again in the middle of the night. In the interests of maintaining dry bedding, one of my parents would wake me up during the night and lead me outside of the tent to take a pee. One such night I was awakened and then escorted outside for this purpose. A full moon shone above the treetops, and was so bright that I could clearly distinguish every bush and tree. I was just about ready to do my duty, when I saw a little spruce tree directly in front of me. I suppose it reminded me of a Christmas tree. In any case, I most certainly did not want to spray it.

I turned to my mom and pleaded, "Don't let me pee on the Kimpa tee." I had not yet learned how to pronounce "Christmas tree".

My family still believes that it was at this moment that I decided to protect little trees and pursue a forestry career.

* * *

During our return trip to Cudworth from Lake Waskesui, we stopped at a department store in Prince Albert. With her children in tow, my mother was bravely trying to do some shopping.

In a prominent display case I spied a charming pink celluloid elephant. It completely captivated me, and I decided that I must have it. My mother was busily chatting with a store clerk, and ignoring me. I impatiently tugged at her dress and began whining. Still she ignored me, and my whining escalated into a genuine tantrum. In a state of frustrated desperation my mother finally bought the elephant for me to shut me up

Once we were back in the car I received a couple of brisk slaps on my rear for my bad behavior. I didn't really care. I had achieved my goal. For many years it was my most treasured toy.

When I turned seventeen, I left home to become a logger in B.C., and never ever saw the pink elephant again.

* * *

It is a good thing that I am able to preserve memories of this family camping trip in 1929 because that was the first and the last time we went to Lake Waskesui. Once the Depression took control of our lives, our treasured family vacations became a thing of the past.

Show Biz

I am not sure why we decided to crank up such a complicated activity. The project required a lot of preparatory work before we were able to breathe life into it.

The year was 1938. Uncle Laurie and his family would soon be leaving Cudworth and moving to a farm about seventy miles away. His oldest children, Verla and Donald, had shared many activities with me in the past, and we wanted to do something special before they left town. Sort of a going-away celebration.

If I remember correctly, I think it was Verla who suggested that we produce a stage play. Here is the way she explained it.

"I think that we are getting too grown up (we were all between eleven and fourteen years old). Why don't we do something different? Something out of the ordinary. Something that we'll remember for a long time."

Without giving her statement too much thought, Donald and I agreed with her.

Verla continued: "I have an idea that you guys just might go along with. I've been reading a story about Robin Hood. I found it very exciting. There are good guys and bad guys, plus plenty of adventure. Kind of like a western movie about cowboys and rustlers, only this story takes place in England. Why don't we put together a stage play about Robin Hood?"

Donald spoke up. "Do you mean something like the Christmas concert that our school organizes in the town hall? Where everybody wears a special costume, and we memorize things to say?"

"Yes, something like that. But we wouldn't have nearly so many actors. Just our cousins and a few close class mates.

"Also, I don't think we should do it for free. We should charge something for admission."

Obviously, Verla had already put some thought into the idea.

She continued, "There'll be many things for us to do . But before we make a list, I want to talk to Mom because we are going to need her help."

The next day Verla talked to Aunt Clara, and then drew up a list of things to do:

1. Location - Her mom didn't want us to have the play in the house, so we would have to use the garage (they had a very large garage). We would have to sweep out spider webs, take out junk and wash the windows. Aunt Clara thought we should place jars of lilac blooms on the window ledges just before the play to hide the smell of oil. Uncle Laurie would supply some planks and boxes to make benches for the audience.

2. Cast -

Robin Hood........................Ralph

Maid Marian........................Verla

Sheriff of Nottingham .....Donald

Friar Tuck...........................Our fattest cousin

Little John...........................Our tallest cousin

She would talk a few of her friends into playing other parts.

3. Script - Verla would start this going and then we would all pitch in.

4. Costumes - Verla would accumulate a whole bunch of used flour sacks from relatives and neighbours, and her mom would dye them forest green. She would then show Verla how to make vests and caps for everyone.

5. Props - We would use green flour sacks sewn together to make a curtain. Aunt Clara would draw an oak tree on a big piece of cardboard to use as a back drop. And we would need rope. All the boys would need bows and arrows. We could make some out of red willow and strong string.

6. Admission - To be collected at the door by Aunt Clara

Pre-school children..................free

School children.........................2 cents each

Adults...5 cents each

7. Signs - We would need four signs:

A - PEANUTS IN THE SHELL.......10 for 1 penny

B - LEMONADE..................................1 glass for 5 cents

C - NO SMOKING (we were ahead of our time)

D - THE END

I think we rehearsed the play only once. Finally, our big day arrived and we prepared to start the show after lunch on a Saturday.

Our audience was made up of many ages. There were three or four pre-school kids, a couple of older cousins, our mothers, our grand parents and some next door neighbours. About fifteen people in all.

As far as I can remember, just about anything that could go wrong, did so. To begin with, the flour sack curtain became stuck. We could not get it to move sideways to open up the view of the stage. Finally, two of us yanked the curtain as hard as we could.

The supporting cord broke and the curtain collapsed on the floor. This resulted in much giggling and laughter from our audience. A couple of the little boys threw peanuts at us.

This swanky opening to our dramatic performance must have shocked the cast severely, because most of us sort of forgot our lines. Instead of just standing there, gaping dumbly at the audience, the boys swaggered around twanging their bowstrings and brandishing their arrows. Most of the girls in the cast just giggled and held their hands in front of their mouths. This state of affairs again produced more mirth from the audience.

Somehow, we managed to convey to the audience that Robin Hood was intent on rescuing Maid Marian from the evil clutches of the Sheriff of Nottingham. It was at this point that I was supposed to swing on a vine from an oak tree, tackle the Sheriff, and take off with Maid Marian.

Instead of a vine, we had fastened an old rope to a rafter of the garage. We had not tested the rope for strength. As I swung through the air "with the greatest of ease" toward the audience, the rope broke. I collapsed on the floor just short of the front bench. The applause was thunderous. This was the final scene. I seem to remember Verla's little sister Noreen waddling across the stage carrying a cardboard sign which read : THE END

Our pleasure did not end at that point in time. We counted up the cash we'd earned - somewhere around fifty cents. Then we hurried to the drug store where we noisily slurped chocolate milk shakes and laughed about our success on the stage.

The next day Grampa Reaser told Verla that our play was the funniest show he had seen since he left Minnesota in 1913.

The Sinking of the Barbarian

Oh, to be a Viking free,
And sail upon the open sea,
In a wind-blown Viking sailing craft
Or just a light weight wooden raft;
That's the life for me.

This verse was the entry in my diary for July 14, 1939. My two cousins, Verla and Donald, and I composed it in honor of a very special summer holiday project. We built a Viking craft on the shore of Lacvert Lake, Saskatchewan.

The lake was nearly a half mile across, and twice that in length. However, it was a very shallow lake, with gobs of yellowish-green, gucky stuff floating around among the reeds near the shore. The lake could more properly have been called a big slough. It was also an exceptionally muddy lake. At the water's edge a fourteen year old boy, like me, would sink almost knee-deep into the gooey, slimy mud. Twenty feet out in the lake, the water was still only a few inches deep. Definitely not the ideal place at which to launch a water craft of any description. But we had no choice. The entire shoreline of this lake was a muddy, murky mess.

The lake was only a couple hundred feet from my uncle's farm yard. I was a visitor, spending my summer holidays enjoying farm life and the companionship of my cousins.

I can't remember who first suggested building a raft. Perhaps there just wasn't anything better to do. In any case, we decided to build a raft, launch it in Lacvert Lake, and pretend that we were blood-thirsty Vikings on the prowl.

The first challenge was to find suitable material for raft construction. Uncle Laurie had built a log chicken house the previous year, and there were sections of small logs left over from the project. We selected a half dozen chunks around six to eight feet long.

Fortunately, we were joined by Louie, a strong teenage neighbour boy. He was a big help in dragging the logs to the lake. For decking, we salvaged some shiplap from the scrap pile behind my uncle's work shop. There was a good supply of nails in the shop so we helped ourselves. Our project was now ready to get under way.

We positioned the logs close together, parallel to one another. We place the longest logs in the middle to give us a "pointy" end.

Before finishing the deck we decided to put up a sail. We found a small diameter pole about six feet long, and nailed it to the end of a log at the bow end of our raft. For stability we attached two guy lines made of binder twine. A piece of canvas between the mast and one guy line served as a sail.

We then decided that we needed a suitable flag if we were going to be Viking pirates. We salvaged a piece of recycled flour sacking from Aunt Clara's rag bag, and Verla used charcoal to draw a skull and crossbones on it. We fastened the flag to the mast. The skull and cross bones added a threatening quality to our craft. The raft was now ready to launch.

As we admired our handiwork, Verla suggested: "I think we should give it a name. All boats get names, you know, like the

Cutty Sark we read about in school."

We all agreed, and decided to first float the raft in the lake before christening it. That's where the serious problems began. The greasy mud at the shoreline provided very limited traction. At first we could barely budge the raft. We struggled and strained and slipped and fell in the gooey mess. It took us nearly twenty minutes to finally float the raft, at which time we were a very sorry-looking, mud-covered crew. Although we had become grimy and slimy, our spirits weren't dampened in the least. We were still determined to become fierce Vikings.

After a brief discussion, we selected a name for our Viking craft. We would call it the *Barbarian* in keeping with blood-thirsty Viking notoriety. Then Verla volunteered to perform the christening ceremony. She had a tin can full of murky lake water ready for the purpose.

Her brother Donald shouted, "You have to go to the front of the raft to do the job properly."

Verla agreed, and waded laboriously toward the pointy end of the raft. On the way, she stubbed her toe on a stick embedded in the mud, and fell flat on her face in the stinky, mucky water. She floundered to her feet, wiped the mud from her face, refilled the can and calmly named our pirate vessel.

Without any further delay the four of us carefully boarded the raft. There were Verla and Donald, Louie, and myself. All together we probably weighed a little over three hundred pounds. The raft immediately settled very low in the water, with maybe a quarter inch of free board. It wallowed dangerously. It could probably safely accommodate only two of us. Since we all wanted to be blood-thirsty Vikings, no one volunteered to disembark.

Using a pole, we carefully shoved off into deeper water. We had covered about ten raft lengths when we suddenly heard exuberant barking from the direction of the farm yard. It was my cousins' pet dog Rover. Apparently, he had just been returned home by a neighbour who had used him to help recover some cattle that had gone astray.

Rover was a rambunctious family dog of many breeds. He was big and weighed nearly one hundred pounds. It took him less than a minute to discover our whereabouts. When he spied us on the raft he immediately jumped into the water to join us. As soon as he arrived at the raft, he joyously clambered aboard. The one hundred pounds he brought with him was more than enough to swamp the raft.

The four of us fell into the water, but somehow Rover managed to maintain his balance, and he now sat up proudly on the raft, the only surviving Viking.

We staggered ashore. We were all wet, very tired and very dirty, so we headed home to get cleaned up. Rover soon joined us.

We didn't try to retrieve the *Barbarian* that day. We had expended too much energy and achieved too little enjoyment in return. The next day a strong wind moved the raft away. We searched along the shore but it was nowhere to be seen.

Perhaps the *Barbarian* landed on some distant shore where it was claimed by bigger, tougher, meaner, stronger Viking pirates.

Part II

ANIMAL STORIES

"We didn't have many material things, but we always had enough to eat." I often heard this comment from old-timers who survived the Depression on a prairie farm.

Raising farm animals was a major contributing factor to that survival. On almost any farm there was usually a steady supply of meat, milk, butter and eggs. During the almost cashless society of the thirties, some of these products were bartered to obtain essentials such as sugar, salt, flour, kerosene etc. There always seemed to be a market for cream, and in many farm households the cream cheque represented the major part of cash income.

Taking care of farm animals was a major job. It was often both tiresome and tedious. Instead of concentrating on stories describing the drudgery and toil of milking, or cleaning barns, or making hay, I tried to highlight whatever humour I could find.

As you can see from the results, some of my stories are rather unusual. For instance, some members of my family think that "Birds of a Feather" is a bit far-fetched. I disagree. The story was told to me by a highly respected old-timer in our Seniors Curling Club. When I told him that my kinfolk had doubts about his story, he was insulted. I heard him mutter something under his breath. I think he said, "Ralph, never let the truth get in the way of a good story."

My advice to the reader is: "Put your tongue in your cheek. Read on and enjoy."

Strictly for the Birds

I have a friend, Bob Johnson, who is of the opinion that chickens are rather filthy birds. He had come to this conclusion nearly sixty years ago while living on a Saskatchewan farm. As a lad he often saw chickens scratching horse droppings in the farm yard, and pecking away on a manure pile in the hope of discovering some undigested grain or insect larvae. These are arguably very unhygenic practices! The following chicken tales are a glowing testament to Bob's story-telling talent.

Bob Johnson was raised on a farm ten miles west of Wilkie, around a hundred miles west of Saskatoon. The nearest neighbours, Tom and Lena S., owned the normal variety of livestock and fowl that one would find on a Saskatchewan farm in those depression days. They kept a flock of over fifty chickens and Lena was responsible for their care. On a daily basis she would feed and water them, and collect freshly laid eggs. Annually she would take steps to reproduce her flock. This entailed careful observation of her hens in order to select a broody one which by its behaviour was interested in raising a family. Having identified such a hen, the housewife would place it in the "maternity" section of the chicken house in a special compartment where she had carefully deposited about fifteen eggs collected earlier. The presence of an over-active rooster assured her that all of these eggs were fertile.

For the benefit of the uninformed it should be noted that a broody hen undergoes changes in behaviour. She struts about in a special halting manner, clucking slowly but almost continuously. In so doing this "clucker" expresses an urge to hatch a clutch of eggs and become a mother.

One spring Lena had just completed the task of selecting and launching a broody hen on a motherhood course, when her two grandsons arrived for a weekend. They were thirteen year old twins, and at times they were downright hellions bent on mischief- making. In fact, her husband often declared, "These boys are a menace to society. They're so full of piss and vinegar".

About a quarter of the farm was still used as a pasture. It had large areas of grassland interspersed with small clusters of trembling aspen or "popple" as some of the old timers called it. The twins decided to explore the more remote portions, which brought them to a distant grove of especially large aspen trees. As they approached the trees, they noticed a chicken hawk flying in circles around the tallest tree. The bird suddenly disappeared and the twins soon spotted a large nest near the top of the tree. They shinnied up the tree to explore. As they neared the nest, the chicken hawk squawked loudly and then took flight. In the nest they discovered two eggs. They suddenly had a brilliant idea. Why not acquire one of these eggs and place it among the chicken eggs being incubated by the broody hen? Carefully they removed one egg from the nest, wrapped it in a handkerchief and safely put it in a shirt pocket.

After they returned to the barnyard, they sneaked into the henhouse, gently lifted the "clucker" and carefully placed the chicken hawk egg among the chicken eggs destined for hatching.

They solemnly agreed not to tell their grandparents of their treachery.

The incubation days flew by quickly, and hatching was soon underway. By the third weekend in April, all the chicks had emerged from their shells. It so happened that the twins arrived at the farm on this particular weekend. They immediately accompanied Lena to the chicken house to visit the baby chicks.

With a bright smile on her face, Lena light-heartedly counted the baby chicks. Her mood immediately changed when she discovered that one of the chicks was quite different from all the others. In comparison to the bright-eyed, cute fuzzy little chicks, the baby hawk looked both awkward and ugly. Instead of chirping a happy, friendly sound like the other baby chicks, the hawklet emitted high-pitched squawks that sounded downright hostile. Lena was shocked at the sight. The twins repressed giggles.

Lena studied the brood for several minutes. She thought, "Maybe this strange chick is a 'throwback', a sort of genetic accident."

Finally she made up her mind. She quickly left the chicken house, stopped at the tool shed to pick up an axe, and went looking for her husband, the twins trailing behind.

"Tom, please take this axe and dispatch the rooster; he is just not doing his job efficiently any more." She then explained her reasoning behind this request. Tom listened attentively, and then headed resolutely toward the chicken house, axe in hand.

When the twins saw their grandfather striding purposefully toward the chopping block by the wood pile, with a struggling and flapping rooster grasped firmly by the legs, they realized that their practical joke had gone too far. Although they were often mischievous brats, they also loved animals and they could not remain silent and let the rooster lose its head on the chopping block. They must do something to rescue this unjustly victimized bird. In one voice they yelled at their grandfather, "This rooster had nothing to do with this weird-looking chick." Then they confessed to robbing the hawk's nest and placing the egg under the brooding hen.

Both Tom and Lena could not keep a straight face. When they started to laugh, the twins joined in. All of them were greatly relieved that the rooster would not be decapitated. No one was more relieved than the rooster.

If you experienced some difficulty in believing this story, you are not alone. Not only that, you will definitely have reality problems with the next story, also told to me by Bob Johnson. He swears that both stories are the truth. If you care to authenticate the veracity of these tales, Bob can be reached by phoning 250-386-639 at the Victoria Curling Club.

The second story about chickens concerns events on another neighbouring farm. This farm had soil of rather poor quality. It was very stony and the topography was challenging, as it had many hills and gullies. Their best crops had been only mediocre, and George and Sylvia O. encountered very hard times soon after the Depression started. In desperation the owner fabricated a still, installed it in dense bush land far from the home site, and produced moonshine.

After a few disappointing batches, he managed to produce a high quality moonshine which he sold to bootleggers in Wilkie.

One day in 1935, on the occasion of their twentieth wedding anniversary, Sylvia commented on the fact that they had never left the farm to take a decent holiday. Right then and there her husband decided to increase his income by expanding production of his "white lightening". It took over a month to accumulate a stock of fifty one-gallon jugs of home brew. He knew that the Mounties were keeping an eye out for bootleggers so he hid the hooch in a manure pile some distance from the house.

The couple simultaneously undertook a separate project to increase the growth of their vacation fund. They built up a flock of chickens and soon produced an abundance of eggs. Prices were low, but they saved every penny from egg sales.

Early one morning a friend living in Wilkie (one of the bootleggers they supplied) phoned and warned the housewife that the Mounties were planning to check their farm for illegal spirits.

Her husband was working in a distant field and would not be home until supper time, so she decided to take immediate action on her own. She grabbed a hammer, ran to the manure pile, and started smashing the gallon jugs full of moonshine. In ten minutes she had disposed of the entire inventory of fifty bottles. Immediately she had misgivings.

She thought to herself: "What if the police don't even come here?"

"What will my husband say? He worked many hours to fill these jugs."

As she walked slowly back to the house a gentle breeze arose from the south. Soon the pungent odour of moonshine-soaked, overproof horse manure wafted steadily toward the farm buildings. The chickens were the first to notice this enticing smell and the entire flock streamed past the barn, heading for the manure pile. Evidently, the pile contained a considerable amount of undigested seeds. The chickens eagerly glutted themselves with these booze-soaked kernels of grain.

Sure enough, the police suddenly appeared and commenced to snoop around. As they approached the manure pile, they also detected the smell of manury moonshine. Then they saw the chickens which had been overcome by alcohol consumption. Every last one had keeled over and passed out, their beaks agape and their feet pointed skyward. Before passing out, the chickens had consumed every last kernel of impregnated grain. There was no longer any evidence. The police realized that they had been outfoxed by drunken birds, and had no alternative but to drive back to town empty-handed.

Sylvia decided to check out the situation at the manure pile. To her horror she saw her beloved birds scattered about in postures so weird that she was convinced that they had died. She decided to immediately prepare their bodies for market in order to salvage a few bucks from this total disaster.

She phoned her neighbor and borrowed two teenaged daughters to help pluck the feathers from the chickens. It took about three hours of hard work before the entire flock was denuded. By this time some of the birds began to recover from their hangovers. One by one they staggered to their feet and headed toward the chicken house, shivering uncontrollably and with beaks chattering violently. For a couple of minutes Sylvia watched this spectacle in shocked amazement, and then fainted.

To aid the recovery of these valuable birds, they were confined to the chicken house where a second heater was soon installed for their comfort. Gradually a new coat of feathers grew in and the hens resumed laying eggs, except for a few who seemed to have developed alcohol withdrawal syndrome.

The illegal production of moonshine was resumed, but a new hiding place was developed far from both the manure pile and the chicken house. Two years later, George and Sylvia successfully celebrated a second honeymoon in Yellowstone Park.

The Case of the Missing Mongrel

This story took place around 1930 on Milton Hawkins farm near Battleford, Saskatchewan. It was written by his son Tom, who is now eighty years old. When you read this, I think you'll agree that Tom writes a great story.

My brother Cliff was a heavy sleeper. In fact it was nearly impossible for any one to get him mobile in the morning to get up and milk the cows and get the chores done unless he had the urge to eat, the chore he managed very well.

We had been having some trouble with a dog invading the chicken house and making off with some of our prize layers. One morning about four-thirty my Dad was awakened by the chickens setting up a fuss. It took some time for him to get Cliff mobile but finally in his underwear and cussing, he grabbed the rifle and approached the farm buildings - just in time to see this yellow dog emerge from the hen house with a chicken. Cliff, thinking to scare the culprit and without taking aim, raised the rifle with one arm and fired. The shot was perfect - we had one dead dog on our hands. What to do? The decision was made to bury the dog - but not near *our* home. I accompanied Cliff to do the deed on a secluded treed part of the neighbour's farm

A couple of days later, Alex McRae came looking for his mutt - saying that he had got up to let the dog out to do its business and he hadn't seen it since - and neither had anyone else.

The Cow with the Crumpled Horn

The colour of the beast is what first attracted my attention. Its coat was mostly off-white, but the upper part of its body sported hundreds of bright pink blotches. It almost looked as though pink paint had been spattered over the animal.

But the real distinguishing feature of this cow was its conspicuous crumpled horn.

The cow's horns were terribly mismatched. The left side of her head supported a very normal-looking horn, about the right size and shape and pointed in the right direction.

The other horn was badly disfigured and much shorter that its partner. It was twisted so severely that the point was aimed forward instead of upward. The horn looked to be an ugly and useless appendage. Not so. In fact, the crumpled horn was used as a versatile tool. It was just the right size and orientation to effortlessly trigger the latch on our front gate.

In a single motion the cow could manipulate the horn to unlatch our front gate and gain entry to our yard.

After dexterously opening the gate, the cow would leisurely amble across the lawn, its hooves punching deep and damaging holes in our lawn. Then as a decorative touch it would pause to leave an odious signature on the grass beside the lilac bush. The cow would then saunter past our house and invade the vegetable garden, usually starting with brunch in the cabbage patch.

Our vegetable garden was a treasured part of Mom's domain. She was the manager who selected the seeds and the planting dates, organized the watering and weeding schedules and directed harvest operations.

This bovine invasion was as much an indignity to her person as it was to the garden itself.

One summer, the crumpled-horn cow raided our garden twice in one week. Mom lost all patience. She decided to stop this invasion once and for all. Her first inclination was to use my father's shotgun and dispatch the animal. But the urge did not last for more than a few seconds because Mom had never broken the law. Instead, she procured a long piece of half inch-rope and hung it on a nail by our back porch.

A few days later the cow returned. My sister saw it dislodge the gate latch with its crumpled horn and make its way across the front lawn. After again contributing some fertilizer near the lilac bush, it headed straight for the cabbage patch, trampling right over the bush beans. My sister ran into the kitchen.

"Mom, that pinkish cow with the funny horn is in our garden again!"

In a flash mom grabbed the rope and headed toward the garden. She had plenty of experience and know-how to carry through with her plan.

As a young teenager, she had moved with her family from a small town in Minnesota to a Saskatchewan farm. She developed into a hard-working farm girl, proficient at housekeeping, baking bread, preparing scrumptious meals, feeding livestock, doing field work during harvest time, and of course, milking cows twice a day.

With the rope draped over one arm, she slowly approached the trespasser as it munched her prize cabbages. In a minute, she secured the rope around the cow's neck and calmly led it out of the garden to a sturdy clothes-line post. She tethered it and fetched a pail from the house. She then applied her milkmaid experience and in 15 minutes the bucket was filled and the cow's udder was bone dry.

She led the cow to the front gate and released her onto the street. She was uncertain if the cow would return, but at least there had been one important short-term benefit: her anger at the cow's invasion had subsided.

The days went by and soon the garden vegetables were harvested.

When the first snowfall dusted the landscape, the cow with the crumpled horn had not reappeared

The next summer, we again raised a luxuriant garden without invasions from the crumpled-horn cow.

Indeed, peace prevailed on our prairie property and we began to wonder what had happened to this unusual animal.

The mystery of its disappearance was solved the next summer when I saw this cow again. Along with ten or fifteen sad-looking cattle, it stood in the stockyard by the railway track awaiting shipment to a Saskatoon slaughter house.

It had definitely consumed its last cabbage.

My Last Weekend at Uncle Laurie's Farm

It was around a week before Christmas in 1942. I had been working at Uncle Laurie's farm since June, following my graduation from high school.

I was in a happy mood. In a few days I would be leaving on the train to join my family for Christmas.

At breakfast on my last Sunday on the farm, Uncle Laurie's brother Oscar gave me an enquiring look and asked, "Ralph, how would you like to be a cowboy today and ride with me to visit Tom Cardiff? I want to talk to him about some work he might do for us."

When he mentioned Tom Cardiff, I vaguely knew who he was talking about, although I had never met him.

Oscar continued: "There are actually three Cardiff brothers, all with a rare assortment of names: Tom, Dick and Harry."

Then he explained that they were all farmers in their fifties. All confirmed bachelors, all living independently and alone on three adjacent farms.

I accepted Oscar's invitation to accompany him. Horseback riding was not my favourite activity, but the outing would be enjoyable. I had never ridden a horse in snowy conditions.

Around 10:00 a.m. we saddled our horses and departed. First, we took a short cut through the pasture, riding in single file on a trail that passed through dense patches of white poplar bush land interspersed with open grassland, now covered by a foot of snow.

It was a bright, crisp, winter day. A soft blue Saskatchewan sky overhead and hard- packed snow underfoot. The horizon was barely visible in the distance and we could see the thousands of acres of stubble-covered field that I had helped harvest a few months previously.

Every branch and twig of the poplars was covered with a thick coat of hoar frost that glistened and sparkled in the sunshine. While riding through this winter wonderland , we disturbed a pair of ruffed grouse which had been resting under a snow cover. In a flash they burst through the snow and took flight sending sprays of snow flying in all directions.

After reaching the highway, we traveled at a slow trot. Oscar did not want the horses to get overheated.

When we turned off the road into Tom's place, I was shocked by the run-down, ramshackled appearance everywhere in view. Decadence and neglect had taken their toll. Piles of ancient farm machinery were scattered under a grove of small white poplar trees. The partial skeleton of an abandoned tractor rusted away near several huge wagon wheels which had fallen apart.

Everything in sight created a dull, depressing appearance. Had it not been for a wispy curl of smoke rising from the chimney, the place would have looked completely abandoned. After entering the house, I realized that not even one brush-full of paint had ever been used inside or outside.

The wretched appearance of everything in the farm yard was in sharp contrast to the personality of the sole inhabitant of this country "estate". I first noticed Tom's bright eyes and his chirpy, positive tone of voice. He was exuberant, friendly and humorous. He bubbled over with conversation. Obviously, he was very happy to have visitors. Perhaps the first for several weeks?

I was surprised to see that Tom was clean shaven. He later mentioned that he shaved every Sunday morning. He rationalized that since he lived too many miles from any church, he would acknowledge this day of the week by shaving and changing clothes. I noticed that he did not say that he changed into clean clothes.

The top of his head was quite bald, and the fringe hair was combed neatly and slicked down with something very shiny. Could it be lard?

The inside wall cladding was three inch tongue and groove - never painted and certainly never washed. These old boards had weathered and absorbed kitchen cooking fumes for many decades. The result was a rich brown colour, almost a mahogany brown, just about like chocolate. The floor was gritty underfoot and probably had never been scrubbed for years (decades?)

After greeting us with big smiles and an enthusiastic hand shake, Tom hurried over to the wood stove, lifted a lid, shoved in three or four pieces of dry poplar, opened the draft, and placed a big kettle of water on the stove.

The kitchen almost reeked in the memory of many meals. In my mind, there was a preponderance of boiled cabbage, fried bacon and strong coffee. Although Tom was bright and friendly, it was difficult for me to work up an appetite in the gloomy, smelly environment of his one-room home. Yes, this big room, perhaps thirty feet by thirty feet, served Tom as kitchen, bedroom, dining room and parlour. It constituted his entire indoor universe.

As I was checking out this place, Tom put on a heavy coat, a fur cap, heavy boots and mittens. Out the door he went and hurried across the yard toward the barn. When he emerged from the barn, he was carrying a manure fork.

I turned toward Oscar, "Can you tell me what he intends to do with that fork?"

Oscar had visited Tom in the past, and he chuckled as he responded, "He's going to retrieve some stimulating refreshment on the occasion of our visit."

We watched through the fly-shitty windows as Tom lined up one corner of the manure pile with an imaginary line of site extending from the horse trough by the well to the far corner of the barn. At the intersection of the manure pile with this line of site, he began to use the manure fork. A half minute later he bent over and reached into the hole that he had excavated in the manure pile. When he straightened up, he had a gallon jug in his grasp, liberally decorated with manure.

He replaced the fork in the barn, rubbed snow on the jug until it sparkled, and approached the house.

As soon as Tom re-entered the house and removed his outdoor clothing, he became our gracious host. The kettle was already singing on the stove. As he prepared the tea, he asked if we would like something to eat with our tea. He said that he had potatoes and beef stew that he could warm up in a hurry. Oscar and I had already noticed the grimy pots and pans piled up in a dish pan. It did not appear that he ever washed his plate and cup which he kept upside down when not in use. I suppose, to keep the flies away. The plate and cup had been white. With years of neglect they were brown with a rusty hue.

As I said, Oscar had been here before. He knew that we would be relatively safe from food poisoning if we confined our intake to tea, crackers, and cheese (using Oscar's pocket knife).

Tom put the cheese and crackers on the table and then poured the steaming hot tea into some big mugs. The mugs did not look clean, but I thought the tea would sort of sterilize them. Tom then uncorked the jug of moonshine and topped up the mugs. A tablespoon of sugar completed the libation.

I was amazed at the enjoyment I got from this reinforced tea. I felt warm and cozy all the way down to my stomach. Simultaneously, a gentle buzz began to develop in my head. We snacked on the cheese and crackers and then enjoyed yet another whopping tea a la Cardiff, before Oscar indicated that we should soon be on our way home. We should get going because there were chores waiting for us.

We mounted our steeds, said good bye to Tom, and trotted briskly back to the main road. I felt great! The temperature was cool, maybe four or five degrees of frost. Pure prairie air. Not a breath of wind. The sun was still a half hour above the horizon. I still had an enjoyable glow from the moonshine.

Suddenly, Oscar whistled sharply and dug his heels into King's sides. King perked his ears, and immediately changed gears to a flat-out gallop. Babe did not require any signal from me. She wanted to race.

Of course, Oscar stayed ahead all the way. He was by far the better rider, and he rode the fastest horse. I stayed about thirty feet behind him. Chunks of hard-packed snow were flung into my face from King's thundering hooves. Oscar turned in his saddle and enjoyed watching me trying to avoid getting hit.

I don't remember how far we raced. I do remember hanging on to the saddle as we galloped down the road.

The events of that Sunday sixty years ago, will always stay with me. Good horses, good friends, good hospitality and a real good time.

Steam-Powered Harvest

What a remarkable cavalcade! It was stretched out over a considerable distance, nearly a thousand feet, as it wheeled slowly down the dirt road. Wispy clouds of dust arose and were suspended for a few moments over this retinue. Leading the procession were two mammoth machines: a steam-powered tractor noisily towing one of the biggest threshing machines ever made. Next in line were eight hay racks each pulled by a team of horses. A huge horse-drawn bunk house on wheels followed. Lagging behind were several wagons equipped with boxes for hauling grain. The crew consisted of twenty individuals, mostly hard-muscled young men. A couple of young boys were included to do some of the lighter work.

The arrival of this unusual procession meant different things to different individuals. To the owner of the farm, it brought anticipation and fulfillment. He knew that his crop would soon be harvested and stored safely in a granary. This huge assembly of men, equipment and horses would thresh his entire crop in less than a week and guarantee that the quality and yield of his grain would not be threatened by unfavourable weather conditions, almost sure to come.

The women of the household, including neighbours' wives and daughters, displayed much less good humour. They knew that they would labour long hours to prepare substantial and appetizing meals for twenty men. In addition to three square meals eaten at the farm house each day, a substantial lunch would be served in the fields in mid-morning and again in the afternoon. And, of course, the women would attend to normal farm chores: milking a half dozen cows twice a day; feeding and watering a great variety of live stock; fetching water for the household plus a dozen smaller tasks.

The animals on the farm also seemed to anticipate the arrival of the threshing outfit and crew. They seemed to display signs of trepidation and concern. The most noticeable were the chickens who clucked nervously as they scratched for food in the barnyard. They seemed to realize that at least a dozen birds were needed to feed twenty hungry harvesters for a single supper. Moreover, chicken would be on the menu several times during the next week. Occasionally a young fat rooster would glance wistfully in the direction of the pens holding the ducks and geese who also began behaving apprehensively .

There appeared to be extra "oinks" of concern emanating from the pig pen. Some of the larger pigs were staring off into the distance contemplating how many dozen pork chops would be devoured to satisfy gargantuan bundle-pitcher appetites.

In a pen just past the big barn, a couple of fattening steers stared nervously at the horizon. Did they realize that four quarters of beef were already hanging in the ice house? They seemed to be missing one of their brethren, and glowered suspiciously in the general direction of the ice house.

Even the dogs and cats were not behaving normally. Instead of curling up in a warm spot and snoozing, the cats were excited, and prowled warily through various sheds and barns. The dogs displayed their agitation by yelping and running helter skelter.

Although I lived in Saskatchewan from 1925 to 1943, I never did see a steam-powered threshing outfit. The background for this story arises entirely from first-hand information from John Nyberg who worked for his father's steam threshing outfit for twelve years.

In 1922 at ten years of age, John became a full time member of the threshing crew. He was called a "straw monkey", and it was his responsibility to transport huge loads of straw to be used as fuel for the steam tractor. He already had experience driving horses. He would park the hay rack under the blower pipe of the threshing machine. When the hay rack was full of straw, he would drive the load to the tractor and unload the straw into a rack near the boiler.

In 1924 John was promoted to the job of "water monkey". He drove a horse drawn tanker wagon to the nearest slough to fetch a load of water for the steam tractor. The tanker was equipped with a hand pump and a long hose which extended into the water. It took at least a half an hour of strenuous pumping to fill the tank.

In 1927 John advanced to the "fireman" position. It was his job to fire up the steam engine at five a.m. and fuel the fire all day long.

In 1930 John became a bundle pitcher. This involved driving a horse-drawn hay rack out into the field, stacking the rack with bundles (sheaves of grain), returning to the threshing machine and feeding the bundles into this greedy monster He was now a hard-muscled young man and he easily coped with the long hours of hard labour.

His father's threshing outfit was an important source of income, especially during the cash-starved depression years. Most of this income was derived by "custom" threshing on neighbouring farms. John recalls that in one year their threshing season extended to fifty consecutive days.

The monstrous steam tractor has long been extinct on the Canadian prairies. A few are captive in several western museums. Occasionally, John will recall the old threshing days, the hissing and puffing of high pressure steam, the clattering reverberations of the threshing machine, the long demanding hours of dusty, sweaty toil, the richness of huge appetizing meals, and a tired but satisfied feeling at the end of the day.

Mackinaw Pockets and Road Apples

I guess I was around ten years old when I made an awesome discovery. That would make it 1935, right in the middle of the Depression.

It happened on my way to my grampa's house, where I would be staying the night. After retiring from the farm to the town of Cudworth, Saskatchewan, Grampa remained active by continuing his medical practice. On top of being a saloon keeper in Minnesota and then a farmer in Saskatchewan, he had been treating sick animals for over forty years.

He called himself a "horse doctor", although he treated any sick four-legged animal. Our family considered him a "medicine man" because he had concocted his own medication for several horse diseases.

I planned to stay overnight at Grampa's house in order to accompany him on a trip to attend a sick horse early the next morning. Grampa would be picked up by a farmer right after breakfast. January blizzards had plugged the roads, making it impossible for Grampa's car.

A big attraction for me was the form of winter transport we would take. For the first time in my life I would be traveling in a horse-drawn caboose.

Most people think that a caboose is a red railway car that tags along at the end of a long freight train. That is a railway caboose used mostly by a brakeman. A second type is a farmer's caboose. It is for use in the winter. It is a little wooden hut mounted on sled runners. A caboose has a front window, benches to sit on and a small wood-burning stove. The occupants are protected from the wind and kept warm by the little stove. Riding out into the countryside in one of these contraptions would be an adventure for me.

I left home right after supper, and walked about five blocks to my Grampa's house. The weather was chilly and windy, so I wore a heavy sweater, a thick woollen mackinaw, a scarf, a toque, and woollen mittens. Most of the time the wind was moderate but occasionally there would be a strong gust that made my eyes water and took my breath away. When this happened, I turned around and walked backwards a few paces to catch my breath.

It was during one of these backward-walking occasions that I made my discovery. I was walking on the hard-packed snow in the middle of the street. As I was walking backwards, I did not see a pile of horse buns, otherwise known as "road apples". My heel dislodged the pile, and one huge road apple rolled free.

It was so big that I whistled in amazement. This was certainly the "mother of all road apples". Perhaps it had been produced by an elephant, I thought. I picked it up, and examined it under the streetlight. It was the biggest and smoothest road apple I had ever seen. It was aerodynamically perfect, and would make a great substitute for a hockey puck when we played street hockey. I could imagine taking a slap shot with it.

Of course, it was frozen solid and very cold. I put this prize in my mackinaw pocket.

Grampa woke me up early the next morning. It was dark outside as we ate our porridge and toast. No sooner had we finished our meal, when the farmer showed up with his horses and caboose.

The ride in the caboose was not as comfortable as I had expected. There were many snow drifts across the road, and the little caboose would pitch sharply as it glided over the top of them.

The farmer had not planned too well. We were a little over half way to our destination when we ran out of firewood. The fire soon went out. The caboose was not well insulated and it became as cold as an ice box.

By the time we arrived at the farm, I was shivering from the cold, despite wearing my heavy mackinaw. Grampa warmed himself by the kitchen stove for a few minutes before accompanying the farmer to attend to the sick animal.

I did not go with them. I was just too cold. Instead, I drew up a chair next to the stove and made myself comfortable, still wearing my mackinaw. Once I got really warm, I drifted off to sleep.

I was still in dreamland when Grampa and the farmer returned to the kitchen. They removed their caps and coats and sat down at the kitchen table. The farmer served Grampa a mug of coffee liberally laced with illegally distilled moonshine. Grampa enjoyed a drink and told the farmer that it warmed the "cockles of his heart". I also sat at the table enjoying a glass of milk and some cookies.

I guess we'd been sitting at the table for some considerable length of time when we simultaneously became aware of an unpleasant, barnyard-type odor. Grampa and the farmer both pointed their noses in the air and sniffed exploringly in all directions. Then they checked their boots, but there was no sign of manure. Again, they sniffed noisily, paused, and then looked accusingly at me.

"Why are you looking at me? I didn't even go near the barn."

They understood the logic of my statement, but their noses still told them that I was the guilty party. I became very uncomfortable. It was so unlike my grampa to embarass me.

I shrugged my shoulders to appear indifferent and dug my hands deeply into the big pockets of my mackinaw - right into something wet and mushy. I dragged a very small handful of whatever it was out of my pocket. The reeking remnants of what had been my trophy road apple dripped from between my fingers.

Grampa and the farmer burst out laughing at a kid who stored manure in his pockets. I didn't think it was too funny. Then Grampa asked, "How did that mess get in your pocket?"

I told him about my discovery of the huge horse bun the night before, and why I had kept it. As I described the situation, I began to realize how funny it was, and I laughed with them.

I had taken off my mackinaw and hung it on the back of a chair. By this time the right hand pocket was dripping brown droplets, and the smell wasn't about to go away any time soon.

The farmer was very grateful that Grampa had fixed his horse. As was the custom in those days of an almost-cashless society, he gave Grampa a gallon of first class moonshine for his services.

On the way back to town in the caboose, I wore a heavy coat that the farmer loaned to me. I slept most of the way home except when the caboose pitched suddenly over the snow drifts. Each time I woke up, I could see a humorous glint in my grampa's eyes.

Snoopy's Grand Tour

During Hugh Cowan's six and ninety years on this earth, he was confronted with more than his share of extraordinary experiences. The exceptionally good memory of his advanced years makes these stories available for our enjoyment.

* * *

Hugh's first memory of special events stems from an incident in 1912 when he was five years old. In that year, his family emigrated from Scotland to Canada in search of a better life. They had booked passage for steerage accommodation because it offered the cheapest transport across the Atlantic.

A month before sailing, they were informed that they would be sailing on board the Titanic. They were delighted by this news. During the past year, the construction of this ship had become a newsworthy event. Many of the newspaper writers had gone into ecstasy describing the luxurious cabins and suites, the elaborate and well-appointed entertainment facilities, the plans for serving gourmet meals, and above all, the absolute assurance that the ship could not possibly sink.

On the day of departure, they boarded a train in Glasgow early in the morning, and arrived at Southampton in mid-afternoon.

Upon arrival at dockside, the Cowan family joined a line-up at the gangplank of the Titanic and, in due time, presented their identification and tickets. The two ship's officers who were processing passengers carefully checked them out, consulted the passenger list, and then nervously spoke to each other in hushed tones. They then informed the Cowan family that their passage on board the Titanic had been cancelled due to over-booking.

The Cowan's were terribly disappointed to miss out on the maiden voyage on this "unsinkable" ship. Later that day, another frustrated passenger suggested that their passage had been cancelled to financially benefit the White Star Shipping Company. Apparently, the demand for passage on the Titanic had grown so rapidly that the company was able to re-book steerage accommodations at a much higher price.

As a gesture of good will, the ship's officers promised to immediately seek passage for the Cowan's on an alterative ship. Ironically, a few days later, they became passengers aboard the Cunard liner Lucitania which three years later was torpedoed and sunk by a German U-boat. The loss of one hundred Americans among the eleven hundred people who perished in this attack contributed toward the U.S.A.'s entry into the war.

When the Cowan family arrived in Halifax, they were greeted with news of the Titanic disaster and counted their blessings.

* * *

Hugh's father immediately found a job on a dairy farm in Ontario. He had hoped to settle in western Canada, but that would have to wait until he could save up some money.

Finally in 1916, the family moved to Alberta where his father managed a sheep ranch near Calgary.

After completing grade eight, Hugh began working for local farmers and ranchers.

One of Hugh's most life-threatening experiences occurred while working on a sheep ranch. One afternoon in late winter, while returning on horseback to the ranch from a trip to town, Hugh was overwhelmed by a blizzard.

It was all so sudden. One minute Hugh was happily riding in sunny, calm weather, the next, the sky was filled with black clouds and a fierce wind was pelting powder snow on him and his horse. Visibility also deteriorated and a complete white-out soon developed. Although it was early afternoon, Hugh could not see more than a few feet in any direction. He was riding cross-country in open-range land so there were no fences or roads to guide him. He completely lost his bearings.

Under the circumstances, he decided to trust the instincts of his horse and gave him free rein. The temperature had fallen well below freezing and the frost turned to ice around the horse's nostrils. The poor animal slowed down markedly as it struggled to breathe through the icy build-up . Hugh realized there was a problem when the animal began to stagger. He dismounted and removed the frost and ice. He felt sorry for his horse, and would gladly have walked leading the animal, but Hugh had no idea which direction to take.

The ice again built up around the horse's nostrils a half hour later, and Hugh again cleared it away. Eventually, the horse came to a halt a few feet from a building. Hugh dismounted and suddenly realized that the structure was the barn on his dad's ranch.

The blizzard continued to rage well into the night. The next morning, Hugh and his brothers rode out to check the livestock which had been caught in the storm.

Disaster had struck. In seeking protection from the cold, the sheep had entered a ravine and ganged up. Other sheep piled up on top of the first arrivals. Their tangled corpses covered a good part of the ravine.

* * *

It is not unusual for Canadians to excel in sports and become professional athletes. However, it is rare indeed to discover someone who has attained professional status in more than one sport. Hugh achieved this distinction long before professionals received big salaries. He still feels that he was born about fifty years too soon.

In 1937, Hugh was approached by a Maple Leaf hockey scout who offered Hugh a contract to play for a farm team. He was offered fifty dollars per month. At the time, Hugh was earning twice this amount in an expanding business. Moreover, he was planning to get married. A pay cheque of fifty dollars a month would not adequately support him and his bride. When he asked for more money, he was refused. The hockey scout told him, "Real good hockey players are a dime a dozen in the prairie provinces."

Sadly, Hugh turned down the opportunity to become a professional.

A year later, he became a professional football player for the Calgary team which preceded the Stampeders. Hugh thought the team might have been called the Broncos. Hugh was big, strong and in excellent physical condition. After several weeks of training and practice, they started their first game against a team from Saskatoon. Just before the game started, the coach took Hugh aside and gave him an extraordinary assignment.

"Hugh, you're a big, strong guy with a good head on your shoulders. You have a promising future ahead of you as a football player, especially on the defensive squad. Today, I want you to deliberately injure the Saskatoon quarterback . Breaking a leg or an arm would be just fine."

Hugh was dismayed by this request. In sports, he had never felt animosity toward opposing teams, certainly not enough to deliberately cause injury. It was definitely not "his cup of tea". During the game, he deliberately avoided the opposing quarterback. He never laid a hand on him. After the game, he turned in his equipment and uniform and never played football again.

Hugh finally achieved professional status in a sport which gave him much enjoyment. He became a professional wrestler.

One day while working out at the YMCA in Calgary, he met Jack Taylor who had won a British Empire Wrestling Championship. The two became good friends and Jack began training Hugh.

In 1938, Hugh got the opportunity to join a wrestling circuit which staged wrestling bouts in Edmonton, Calgary, Lethbridge, Saskatoon and Regina. He enjoyed the action but found the pay miserable. During the depression, many wrestling fans could not afford the price of admission to wrestling matches. Consequently, remuneration varied a great deal. The most that Hugh ever earned was fifty dollars for an evening. Frequently, poor attendance resulted in no pay at all.

Hugh's wrestling career came to an end when he joined the Canadian Navy in 1941. While stationed in Victoria, Hugh participated as a wrestler at a benefit promoting the sale of War Bonds.

* * *

Yes, Hugh excelled in several sports. Unfortunately, he also achieved a top rating in sea sickness. There were times when on North Pacific patrol during his navy career that he came very close to jumping overboard to end his misery.

For many years, he had been aware of a very queasy stomach He had first discovered this weakness during a duck hunting trip in Alberta. He and his partner had shot several ducks. Some of the dead birds were floating on a shallow slough. Hugh decided to row in a small boat to retrieve the birds. There wasn't a breath of wind. Not even a ripple on the water. Despite the absolute calm, Hugh's stomach misbehaved and he upchucked right after picking up the birds.

Although he had a very sensitive stomach, Hugh had joined the Navy, but under unusual circumstances. He had initially joined the R.C.A.F. but became bitterly disappointed when months passed without receiving any follow-up instructions from the R.C.A.F.

One day, he met an old friend who was in the Navy. Hugh told him about his frustration with the R.C.A.F. His friend replied, "If you want some action, join the R.C.N. I can get you transferred in two days."

Hugh immediately acted on his friend's advice and became a sailor without giving a second thought to his irritable stomach.

This error in judgment caused him a lot of grief. He experienced sea sickness during every patrol trip along the B.C and Alaska coast. His sharpest memory of rough seas arose during a patrol near the Aleutian Islands. His ship had been tied up for a few days at Dutch Harbor, a major U.S. military base which had been bombed by Japanese planes. The ship was scheduled to leave port and resume patrol toward Prince Rupert. As the ship left port, the crew observed a flurry of activity on a nearby U.S. ship which vigorously displayed a series of signal flags.

Their flags indicated a storm warning and advised the Canadian ship to remain in port. Unfortunately, the flag signals were not read correctly by the Canadian crew and they headed out to sea. Gale force winds soon set in and a severe storm developed. The captain managed to navigate the ship to the lee side of an island where he dropped two anchors in the hope of weathering the storm. Fortunately, the anchors held and after about twenty hours they were able to continue the patrol.

While working in the engine room atmosphere , Hugh would invariably become sea sick. Immediately after completing a shift, he would dress warmly and rush up to the deck to enjoy fresh air and recuperate. To keep warm, he would curl up between a bulkhead and the funnel.

As Christmas approached in 1943, the ship's company decided to celebrate the holiday season with roast turkey and all the trimmings. The ship stopped briefly at a small port in the Alaska panhandle and the cook went shopping to purchase turkeys and other Christmas goodies.

While ashore, he also purchased a couple of bottles of rum and managed to smuggle these aboard. It was Christmas Eve, and he consumed his entire rum supply. The next day, he was in no condition to prepare Christmas dinner. There would be no fancy banquet unless a substitute cook could be found. Hugh immediately volunteered.

He had learned to cook roast turkey in the middle of the depression. Around 1937, Hugh's father had raised a flock of turkeys to augment an almost invisible family income. The turkeys were in good shape in early December. However, the price for turkeys fell drastically. The Cowan family decided to consume the birds instead of selling them at a big loss. The family rose to the occasion and canned all the turkeys in two-quart sealers. After detailed instructions from his mother, Hugh took on the job as chief turkey-cooker.

The results were most gratifying. Hugh produced a delicious product which was subsequently enjoyed at least once a week for an entire year.

* * *

Interesting and colourful events punctuated Hugh's life, even as he approached his ninetieth birthday. One morning, Hugh went out the front door to fetch the news paper. It was a bright and sunny day, and he paused to enjoy the fresh air and flowers in his garden. Suddenly, he experienced a strange feeling. He realized that something was amiss. What was it? He looked closely at his array of lawn ornaments. The four white ducks and the little black duck were still lined up near the edge of the lawn...but where was Snoopy? This little plywood dog resembling the one in the Peanuts cartoon was a favourite of all the neighbours. Hugh had used paint to give it a personality of distinction.

Hugh made a careful search of the front yard, but could not find the little pet. Obviously, someone had stolen it. Hugh felt that he had lost a good friend.

About a month later, the postman delivered a surprise. It was an envelope sent from Belgium, containing only a photograph of a grand building in Bruges. In the foreground, was a young lady cuddling Snoopy in her arms. A week later, a similar photo appeared from Vimy Ridge in France. Again, Snoopy occupied the foreground in the arms of a different young lady. In the course of the next few months, seven more similar letters arrived from as far away as Turkey and Greece. Hugh was happy to see that Snoopy was enjoying many different places.

Then the letters stopped coming. A month later, Snoopy again appeared in Hugh's front yard. To this day Hugh has no idea who meddled with his dog.

Hugh's final comment on this episode of his life was, "I sure wish that the perpetrator would let me know his identity pretty soon. I'd like to find out before I die. I'm ninety-six now. I don't know if I'll make it much past one hundred years."

Part III

TOUGH TIMES

For many Canadians, the years of the Great Depression were "tough times" indeed. As a consequence, I experienced no difficulty in uncovering stories of people who faced the harsh realities of poverty and desperate circumstances.

Including only sad stories would surely overwhelm the reader. Who wants to read only stories which are focused entirely on disaster and tragedy? I wanted a more balanced approach. I decided to point the reader in a different direction, and I did my best to weave a thread or two of humor throughout the fabric of otherwise miserable stories.

In so doing, I really don't expect to generate outright laughter. However, if even a slight grin appears on your face halfway through this chapter, I will consider that my goal was achieved.

Sit Up and Take Notice

This story was told to me by a fellow senior curler, Irwin Shaw. He got the story from his father who served as a councillor in the Weyburn City Hall for several years during the depression. His father was one of the committee members who addressed this young lady's plea for relief.

Desperate circumstances caused by the Great Depression often produced situations of great stress and suffering. A young woman in Weyburn, Saskatchewan would certainly agree with this statement. In 1935, when the entire country was well into the depression, Mary Frame, who was in her mid-thirties, found herself in a destitute state.

Four months previously, in early June, her husband had left on a freight train in search of a job. He left Mary with their four small children to care for, and only a few dollars. She spent all the money on necessities. With winter fast approaching, she knew she would have to get help in order to survive.

Her neighbour told Mary about applying for relief at City Hall. She warned Mary to be prepared for a tough fight. Relief money was in short supply and the city was careful to dole it out only to those in dire need. On hearing this advice, Mary thought of the plight of her four little ones, and resolved to adopt any tactics in order to get help.

On the day that Mary arrived at City Hall to plead her case, she was told to sit in a waiting room. She would be told when the relief committee could see her. The waiting room was small and gloomy. It had seats for a dozen people, and most of these were already occupied when Mary arrived. She settled in for a long wait. Nearly two hours later her turn finally arrived, and she was ushered into the committee room where she would make her plea for help.

The three councillors seated behind a massive table appeared both stern and disinterested. They had already heard several heart-breaking stories that morning and had become both exhausted and depressed. They had lost their concentration. They hardly noticed the young woman who now appeared before them, even though she had taken pains to put on an appropriate appearance. She was neatly dressed. She wore no make-up. Her clothes were clean and unwrinkled. Her hair was tidy. However, if you looked intently, you could see that her jacket was threadbare, and her shoes had definitely seen better days.

At first, Mary tried to make her case by complaining about her hardships. She thought that this approach might evoke a feeling of compassion from the committee members. With tears in her eyes she told them that her husband had left four months ago on a freight train in search of work. She had not heard from him since. She had no idea where he was.

With so many children to take care of, she was unable to seek full time employment. She admitted that she did earn a little money by scrubbing floors in the neighbourhood. This money provided only a few essentials. She told them that she had already sold her best clothing and had even pawned her watch and wedding ring.

After she ended her plea for help she paused for a moment to assess her chances of acceptance. She darted a penetrating glance at the row of stern faces in front of her. She could detect no response. They all sat motionless with a glazed look in their eyes. Not one member displayed a flicker of interest or emotion. Not one seemed to realize just how desperate she was. They appeared totally bored. They had heard it all before. Many times. Instinctively, she knew that she had not made her case.

She quickly came to the conclusion that she would have to use her "back-up plan".

While still seated she said, "Gentlemen, in order to make my situation clear, I have something special to tell you and show you. I realize that in many instances it is difficult for a woman to prove that she is in dire need of relief . I cannot prove that my children are nearly starving unless you visit my home at mealtime. Nor can I convince you that I need fuel to heat my home unless you would visit me and feel the cold. However, I can offer you absolute proof that I am in desperate need."

Somewhat shakily she rose from her chair, her face strained and her fingers clenched. She took a small step forward and coughed slightly to clear her throat. As she began to speak she noted that the committee members began to look at her with more expression in their eyes.

She straightened her posture and stretched to her full height. She then raised both the tone and volume of her voice several notches and declared in a strong, shrill voice, "Gentlemen, I must tell you that I am so damned hard up that I cannot even afford to buy underwear!"

As this remark echoed through the chamber at City Hall, she lifted her dress, and scoffed it over her head, prominently displaying her femininity. The committee members, all male, indeed sat up and took notice. In no time at all she was given approval for the maximum level of relief

In a few minutes she strutted down the corridor of City Hall with a triumphant gleam in her eyes. She halted and stepped briefly into the LADIES room where she donned her panties and bra which she had stowed in her handbag before entering the committee room.

Grandma Kellogg - and Charlie

During the Depression Charlie Stacey and his family lived on a farm in the Saskatchewan dust bowl. This farm was located near Cravel about fifty miles southwest of Moose Jaw. To call it an unproductive farm would be an understatement. Starting in the early 1930's there had been an unbroken succession of crop failures which continued on into the 1940's.

I met Charlie's son Bill in 1999, when the challenging days of the Depression were only a distant memory. Nevertheless, Bill still recalled in detail how the family learned to cope with the hardships of the Depression. In particular, he remembers how Grandma Kellogg helped Charlie raise a family despite desperate circumstances.

Although Charlie was a highly motivated person who worked long and hard to keep the farm going, it was really Grandma Kellogg who gave the family a feeling of stability and security.

Here are some of Bill's memories which illustrate Grandma Kellogg's role as the real head of the family.

* * *

Despite several attempts at digging a well on the farm, the water always turned out to be very alkaline, so much so, that it was unfit for man or beast. There were several sloughs nearby which provided water for livestock; however, the household water had to be hauled from a neighbour's well a half mile distant. It took a half a day for Charlie to complete the circuit with a team of horses and a special water wagon.

One evening after the supper dishes were washed and stacked in the cupboard, after the children were tucked in bed and treated with a bed-time story, after the evening milking had been whirred through the separator, Grandma Kellogg sat down with her son-in-law Charlie to enjoy a relaxing cup of tea.

It was apparent to Charlie that Grandma had something on her mind. There was a special sparkle in her eye and a determined set to her jaw. And there was an almost amiable quality to her voice as she spoke.

"Charlie, I've decided that in the interests of improving our lot in life, I'm going to make a few changes around here."

Charlie thought to himself, "Oh, oh. She's got that fertile mind working overtime again. But I'll be happy to support her idea, as long as it doesn't make more work for me."

Seeing the expression on his face, Grandma continued: "Charlie, since you are forced to haul water so far, and so often, I've always tried to be careful and avoid wasting water. But I've suddenly realised that I do waste water. Quite a bit of it." She continued. "So, after giving the matter some thought, I've decided to change my ways. Maybe I'll be able to conserve a considerable amount of water. I won't elaborate on the details right now, or you'll probably laugh at me. However, I'll demonstrate my new approach this coming weekend, and then you can judge for yourself." Having said her piece, she returned to sipping her tea.

The next Saturday night the first phase of her conservation plan was launched. The custom was for all family members to have their weekly bath on Saturday nights. That activity would not change one iota. The event would take place, one person after another, in a galvanized wash tub in the middle of the kitchen floor.

By the time the entire family and the dog (bathed last) had finished, the bath water was as murky as a slough during a cloud burst.

On Sunday mornings it had always been Charlie's job to dump out the much-used bath water. But no longer! Instead, Grandma Kellogg's plan went into action. The bathwater had settled over night and a thick sludge of grit and grime covered the bottom of the wash tub.

Grandma carefully dipped out the almost clear water on top, and poured it into two huge copper boilers on the cook stove where the water could slowly heat up.

Monday had always been wash-day, and Grandma conformed to that schedule. First thing after breakfast, after the dishes were washed and put away, after lunches had been made and the children had left for school, after the morning milk had been separated, she rolled up her sleeves and started to do the laundry using the water in the copper boilers. She brought out the scrub board and homemade lye soap and got to work

By lunch time, the wash had been completed and Grandma had a crick in her back. But did she discard the soapy, scummy, grimy wash water? No way! Not on your life! Instead, she asked her grand children to bring two sprinkling cans to the kitchen where they were carefully filled with the soapy wash water. First, they watered the tomato plants, then the cucumbers, then the lettuce, then the peas, and so on.

Charlie was fascinated by Grandma Kellogg's approach to water conservation. Her ingenuity and energy had been impressive. Now it appeared that she had fulfilled her objective.

"And she hardly wasted a drop of water." Charlie commented to no one in particular.

But, had Grandma really completed her plan? Not on your life!

Charlie had not observed all of Grandmas' actions. He had failed to notice that just before filling the sprinkling cans, she had dipped a couple of gallons of water into a pail and placed it on the stove.

After this much-used water had achieved the desired temperature, she carefully hoisted it from the stove, and placed it on the kitchen floor. From a cupboard she obtained a scrub brush, a large household rag, and a bar of homemade soap. She groaned with her back pain as she lowered herself to her knees. In a few seconds she started to vigorously scrub the well-worn linoleum.

It took her about a half an hour to complete the job. She slowly stood erect, straightened her back, and sighed with relief. Then she tested the temperature of the water with her finger, carried the pail outside and carefully poured the water on her much treasured pansy bed.

In later years, Grandma Kellogg referred to her water conservation effort as her method of "sequential water use".

* * *

One day Charlie was returning home on horseback from a trip to town where he had gone for spare parts to repair the binder. A couple of miles from home he stopped to visit a friend. It so happened that this farmer had recently started an illegal moonshine operation to help make ends meet.

Charlie consumed several drinks of this home-made alcohol and enjoyed a good visit with this neighbour before mounting his horse to return home. The booze soon took its effect and he began swaying dangerously in the saddle. When he arrived home he was in a complete daze. Of its own accord the horse stopped in front of the house, and in slow motion Charlie gently tumbled out of the saddle into Grandma Kellogg's pansy bed. His undignified dismount was witnessed by Grandma Kellogg as she returned to the house from the vegetable garden. She walked over to him as he lay sprawled on her flower bed. His eyes were closed and he was moaning softly. She gazed down at him. It was not a pretty sight. The front of his jacket was spotted with vomit, and an intermittent drooling slobbered from the corner of his mouth and ran down his neck.

She sighed, then snorted with displeasure and muttered to her unhearing son-in-law, "You're going to need a bath real soon, even if it isn't Saturday. By no means am I letting you into my house in this condition. There's no way I'll allow my place to get messed up by the likes of you."

She asked the children to bring out Charlie's captain's chair from the kitchen. Then they helped her to drag him to the chair from the pansy bed, where they propped him up and bundled him up in an old quilt. As an afterthought, she brought out the slop bucket from the kitchen and placed it near Charlie.

All this jostling about partially roused the woozy Charlie who became very sick, trying desperately to hit the bucket to please Grandma. During the night he suffered from the cold, but did manage to completely empty his stomach. However, when he opened his eyes at dawn he experienced a terrible shock. He could not see! Apparently the novice moonshiner had inadvertently continued the distillation process too long and some fusel oil had also condensed. Charlie spent a miserable couple of weeks of blindness before his sight gradually returned.

While convalescing he met a farm machinery agent who taught him how to conduct a homespun test of moonshine purity. You poured around a half teaspoon of moonshine in the palm of your hand. You then vigorously rubbed it with your other palm. If the rubbing action produced foam, the booze was definitely unfit for human consumption. This test was of little use to Charlie because he never again drank the stuff!

* * *

It was well-known that Charlie was accident prone. Not only did he sometimes cause damage to his own person, but occasionally he was unwittingly the cause of harm to others. To this day his son Bill displays a souvenir of this personal characteristic.

Sixty seven years ago when Bill was only three years old, he was sitting on their front porch watching Charlie construct a rocking chair for Grandma. He was sawing a small recess in one of the rockers to accommodate a chair leg. Just as Bill reached out to pick up a little block of wood from the floor near the chair Charlie was sawing into, the saw slipped and Bill immediately let out a howl, and stuck his finger in his mouth. Soon there was blood all over the place, especially on Bill's face, hands and shirt. Charlie was horrified. "Oh, my God! Let me see! Let me see your hand!"

Bill pulled the injured digit from his mouth. Half an inch of his little finger was missing. Grandma Kellogg , hearing all the commotion, came hurrying out. She took a careful look at Bill's finger and bound it tightly with bandages. She turned and spoke sharply to Charlie. " Get over to the neighbour's place and phone the doctor. I'm certain Bill's finger will need a couple of stitches. Hurry!"

Charlie quickly saddled a horse and took off. Luckily, the doctor was at home, and he promised to come out without delay. It would take a couple of hours to reach their farm traveling by horse and buggy.

It so happened that the doctor enjoyed a drink or two, or even more, of moonshine. On the way to the farm he visited a bootlegger and purchased a quart. By the time he arrived at the farm, he was well into his cups. However, he still had his wits about him. But he was no longer capable of stitching the end of Bill's little finger. (The detached tip of his finger could not be found amongst the sawdust and shavings at the worksite. However, sharp-eyed Grandma Kellogg noticed that the dog displayed a satisfied expression on its face as he licked his chops).

The doctor realized that he would have to convince Grandma Kellogg to sew up Bill's finger.

"Grandma, have you ever done any stitching before?"

She replied, with a touch of humour in her voice, "Of course I have, especially when quilting or patching. Many years ago, I made a dress. It didn't fit so I gave it up."

The doctor continued, with a little smile on his face, "Well, at least you know how to use a needle and thread."

And then the doctor gave her more detailed instructions. Grandma Kellogg displayed a hidden talent, and the job was completed in a few minutes.

Many years later, Bill could still remember being called a brave little soldier for not making a fuss during this home-grown surgery.

* * *

Grandma Kellogg did most of the milking, usually two or three cows. In the summer she would milk outside in the milking yard where she often had to put up with mosquitoes and flies. When these insects became too abundant, she would light up a smudge fire. There were times when she wasn't sure which was the most obnoxious, the thick clouds of smoke or the hordes of insects. In the winter, the weather was too cold so she milked in the barn where there was no smoke and no bugs.

One year, for no apparent reason, the rat population suddenly exploded. After the first snowfall, most of the rats were attracted to the barn which was occupied by horses and cows. The body heat of these animals maintained a higher temperature than any other farm building.

One wintry morning, when Grandma Kellogg was halfway through the milking operation, she became aware of several small ghostly figures moving in the stall. They were difficult to identify in the dim light of the kerosene lantern.

After peering intently into the gloom, she suddenly realized that at least a dozen rats were scurrying about. She jumped up immediately from her milking stool, spilling the milk in the process.

At the top of her voice she screamed, "Charlie! Charlie, get over here! Help me!"

Charlie was working at the far end of the barn, but he heard her voice clearly. He hurried toward Grandma with a pitch fork in his hand. "What's the problem?"

"Rats! Lottsa rats! Hundreds of rats!" she gasped. "All over the goldarn place. I hate rats. If something isn't done about them, you'll have to do all the milking. I'll never go near the barn again!"

Her threat was a serious matter. Not only did Charlie hate milking; he really didn't have the time. Taking care of livestock, feeding, watering, bedding them, and cleaning the stalls was all that he could handle before breakfast. He would have to do something drastic about getting rid of the rats.

True to form Charlie's solution to this problem was out of the ordinary. He constructed a box-like trap with a spring-loaded door triggered by a baited lever. This contraption was baited with table scraps. On the very first night he live-trapped a rat. He then dunked this rat several times in a thick calcimine slurry, and after the animal had dried off, it was released in the barn. True to his expectations, this white rat scared the hell out of the rat population which soon fled down the road to a neighbouring farm.

After this success Grandma resumed her quiet enjoyment of life during milking time, and gradually took a liking to a rat with a fading white coat who had established his turf near the manger, with its beady black eyes fixed on Grandma's pulsating fingers.

* * *

When Bill finished telling this story, he took a deep breath and sighed, "If I thought about it for a while I could remember more stories about my Grandma, but I think that I have fed you the ones that appealed to me most. My Grandma and my father both did their best under difficult circumstances and they did it with love and good humour."

"I cannot imagine what my childhood would have been like without Grandma Kellogg." he said. "She was a very clever woman. She did a lot of strange things ; with her in charge there was seldom a dull moment. I believe she wanted to divert our attention from the tragedy of the Depression. She wanted to give us a normal life."

Coming of Age in Flin Flon

Unlike thousands of others, the Nyberg family did not suffer during the Depression. The energy and abilities of Andrew Nyberg made this possible.

When he emigrated to Canada from Sweden in 1913, he was already an experienced woodsman, and he applied his skills north-west of Prince Albert, Saskatchewan. Upon his arrival there, he immediately contracted a job making railway ties. This "tie-hacking" job was on a "piece work" basis. Since he was already skilled at using a broad axe, he became the top wage earner in the logging camp.

When the work ended in the spring he built a first-class log house, sold it, and earned a substantial profit.

By 1920 he had accumulated enough savings to buy a farm. Two years later he built a sawmill. Then he bought a livery stable in Canwood and operated a profitable bootleg business on the side. Andrew continued to expand his "industrial empire" and bought a steam-powered tractor and a big threshing machine. By threshing for farmers over a large rural area, he increased his income substantially. He then invented and built a machine for cutting tamarack shakes, and added this to his sawmill.

As they grew up, Andrew's three sons became essential parts of this diversified and profitable enterprise. Although the sons were treated with kindness and generosity by their father, there never was any question as to who was the boss. Andrew ran the entire operation almost like a military unit. He made all the important decisions.

When he reached the age of twenty-three, the oldest son, John, decided to leave the security of his home and strike out on his own.

Here is John's story about learning to cope with the Depression after leaving the protection of his family.

* * *

The year was 1935. I got itchy feet. I had worked long enough under my father's supervision. I wanted to strike out on my own, and make my own decisions.

I had heard that there were lots of jobs in the Flin Flon mines near the Saskatchewan-Manitoba border. A neighbour's son, Ralph, an experienced carpenter also wanted to find work away from home. We decided to travel to Flin Flon together.

When I told my father of my plans, he shrugged his shoulders and snickered, " John, you'll never make it on your own. You won't earn enough money to pay for your food. You'll return home in two weeks, and you'll come back with no money in your pocket."

Despite my father's pessimism, I left home with a feeling of hope and enthusiasm, anxious to see what Flin Flon had to offer.

Upon our arrival in Flin Flon we immediately faced major disappointments. Flin Flon was one of the few places in Canada during the Depression, where there were a lot of jobs paying a decent wage. Now, we discovered that all of these mining jobs were filled. Not only that, but there were hundreds of unemployed workers walking the streets, desperately waiting for an opening in the mines.

Even worse news, was the information that the mining company refused to hire any Swedes or Norwegians. Apparently, Nordic miners had instigated a strike a couple of years previously. Anyone would recognize my Swedish surname. I would not be able to find a job in the mine. Would I be able to find work elsewhere in Flin Flon? Maybe my father was right. Maybe I would go home broke. I resolved to prove that he was wrong. I vowed to accept any kind of work that I could find. I would show my father that I could succeed on my own.

There was even more bad news. It was nearly impossible to find a place to rent. Luckily, my partner Ralph met a local resident that he had previously known. For five dollars a month this person rented us a tent and allowed us to set it up in his front yard.

Can you imagine spending the winter in a tent in this northern climate? Actually, it turned out to be a fairly comfortable home. We cut and split a couple of cords of dry firewood from an area where the trees had been killed by a forest fire. Then we bought an air-tight stove and set it up in our tent.

There was no heat in the tent during the day when we were either working or looking for work. Around supper time we would return to our little canvas home and light a fire. In a few minutes our place would warm up and we would prepare supper. During the night one of us would get up and stoke the fire. Our home would be warm when we dressed and prepared our breakfast.

I soon discovered that work was as scarce as hen's teeth. After several days of fruitless searching I stumbled onto a bazaar means of employment. Behind a restaurant in the main street there was a small building which housed a "social club". In reality it was a poker den and bootlegging joint. To attract gambling customers, the owner tried to create the impression that serious gambling was busily underway early in the afternoon. To achieve this, he hired me and a few other unemployed men to play poker using management poker chips. As genuine gamblers arrived, the hired players gave up their seats at the table. We were paid only twenty-five cents for the afternoon, plus a bowl of soup and a sandwich. It proved to be the "easiest money" that I would ever earn in Flin Flon.

Then I discovered that cutting and hauling firewood presented an opportunity to make money at almost any time. I would trek out into the forest, cut poles and then hire a team of horses to deliver the wood in town for a dollar fifty. The total effort took two days and I had to pay fifty cents to rent the horses and a sled.

I would always follow up the slightest rumor of a potential job. On one occasion, I heard that an excavation would be prepared for the construction of a bank building. I got up early and arrived at the site before dawn. My diligence paid off and I worked for a whole week at a decent wage. The foreman in charge of this job liked my performance and attitude. When the job was completed he took me aside and told me about another job opportunity.

A friend of his owned a transport company, and one of his employees was leaving for health reasons. I immediately contacted the owner and applied for the job. It took him a day to check my references and then he hired me.

It was fortunate that I had plenty of experience handling horses on my father's farm. The transport company used horses exclusively: wagons in summer and sleds in winter. Most of the work entailed unloading merchandise from railway cars and delivering it to various business establishments. Sometimes the reverse took place and we hauled tamarack cordwood from the country to the railway for shipment elsewhere.

I was paid thirty cents an hour, a substantial wage for that time. I could now afford better housing. I joined forces with three fellow workers and we rented a comfortable house together.

In November I discovered that my employer also had a contract with the Federal Government to deliver supplies to distant native communities in the hinterland. My boss asked me if I would like to try out one of the shortest delivery trips, and I agreed. The trip would take two days to get to the community and two days to return to Flin Flon.

The weather was not extreme when I left town with a heavily laden sled and a team of horses. In the afternoon the wind picked up and it started to snow. I made camp as darkness fell. I unhitched the horses, strapped a blanket on each one and gave them some hay. I made a primitive lean-to shelter for myself by attaching a canvas tarpaulin to the top of the freight box. By this time, the wind was very strong. I could not light a fire. I ate some half frozen sandwiches and bundled myself in several blankets.

By the next morning the wind had died down and I made good time all day. At dusk I arrived at the native settlement and was given a hearty welcome.

These backwoods people seldom got visitors, especially during the winter. They tried their best to make me feel at home. They served a delicious moose stew and fresh baked bannock. I was exhausted and slept like a log in the corner of one of the cabins.

Early the next morning I left on my return trip. Again the weather did not cooperate and by the time that I arrived at Flin Flon I decided that delivering supplies to distant places in the middle of winter was not for me.

The next day, my boss told me that he was happy with my work and offered to send me on a much longer trip to make a delivery to a community at Reindeer Lake, over a hundred miles away. The round trip would take several weeks - depending on the weather.

I began thinking of the hardships I had just experienced on a very short trip. When my boss saw my hesitation, he said, "I really need you for this job. If you refuse to go I'll have to reduce your working hours to just three days per week."

I decided that it was time to say good-bye to Flin Flon where I had struggled so hard to make a living. I would quit my job and return home. I had been away from my family for nearly two years and I would enjoy seeing them again. Then I remembered my father's reproach when I left. I would show him that I had succeeded on my own. I had saved nearly three hundred dollars. On the way home, I stopped in Prince Albert and purchased a new wardrobe: dress shoes, a suit, shirts, socks, ties and a new overcoat. I would look prosperous when I walked into my dad's house.

I was happy to see my family again and they welcomed me warmly, commenting on my new clothes. Mom served a real feast.

When I again took up my former responsibilities on the farm, I expected to become content. During the first month or two I was very satisfied with my daily life on the farm or in the sawmill. However, I gradually realized that there was something lacking. It was too easy. There was so little challenge. Certainly not like my Flin Flon days where almost every day I had to face a new obstacle, and hustle to make a living. Finally, in early 1939 the wanderlust again captured my spirit and I took the train to Vancouver to seek employment in a milder climate. When I stepped aboard I had much more confidence than when I had left for Flin Flon.

Upon my arrival in Vancouver, I discovered that I was again in the land of the unemployed. Perhaps my Flin Flon experiences would now pay off. In that far away mining town I had learned how to look for work, how to compete for a job, and how to keep it. In rapid succession, I worked as a faller in a logging camp, in a plumbing repair business, as a car mechanic, as a salesman and several other temporary jobs. I never experienced a period of unemployment.

Gradually, I began to realize that owning and operating a business could produce more security than being a wage earner working for somebody else. I saw an opportunity for me to own my own garage business and I went for it. Twenty-five years later I was able to retire on a very comfortable income.

Despite my father's negative prognostication so many years ago, I had truly made it on my own.

The Final Straw

Even his dearest friends and closest neighbours could not agree on the reasons for Zeb's suicide. Some of them expressed the view that no one could possibly take his own life unless he was mentally disturbed. However, the majority believed that he had been mentally sound right to the end. They were convinced that there were compelling reasons which had forced him to the brink. They believed that the hardships of the Depression accompanied by long-suffered physical pain had motivated his decision to end it once and for all.

Then there were a few very embittered individuals who were convinced that the blame for his suicide rested entirely upon the shoulders of the management of the Canadian Pacific Railroad. You just might agree with them after you've read this story.

Soon after World War I, Zeb left an Ontario farm to take up homesteading north of Battleford, Saskatchewan. His father helped him get established by providing money to build a house and barn, and to acquire machinery and livestock. Four years later Zeb married the local school teacher.

They prospered during the 1920's, and five children joined the household. The crops were good and so were grain prices. In 1927, Zeb bought a brand new Chevrolet sedan, and then started to save money toward buying a tractor.

Then the Great Depression hit. And Zeb never did get his tractor.

As the Depression made itself felt on the prairie farmers, Zeb soon realized that mixed farming seemed to be a more successful enterprise than trying to produce only grain. He decided to increase his production of livestock, especially pigs.

Suddenly, in the summer of 1931, tragedy struck. Zeb was thrown from a bucking horse that he was breaking in, and he suffered a severe neck injury. The doctor in Battleford could not help him very much, other than to advise him to wear a wide leather collar to restrict his movements.

He traveled by rail to Saskatoon and visited two specialists and a physiotherapist. Although he got some temporary relief, he still suffered almost continuous pain.

The growing conditions in the summer of 1935 were almost ideal for his crops and Zeb rallied. There was no shortage of rain or sunshine. By mid-July it was apparent that a bumper crop was developing. Then, as can happen all too often on the prairies, a hail storm rolled over the land and destroyed most of his very promising crop. He had been too broke to purchase hail insurance that year.

Only one field of oats escaped damage. He would need at least half of this crop to feed livestock. At harvest time he decided to sell one third of the oats to pay off debts and to buy seed grain next spring.

Usually, he sold his grain to a local grain buyer, but this time he thought he could save money by loading a box car and shipping his oats to market by rail.

It turned out to be a bad choice. While his load of oats was in transit on the railway, the price of oats fell. The railway company informed him that the cost of freight now exceeded the value of his oats. Zeb immediately received a bill demanding payment of the balance owing. There was no money to send.

Without fail, a freight bill, with accrued interest, would arrive every week. Zeb's life began to change about a month after receiving the first bill. The pain in his neck seemed to intensify every time he thought about his growing debt.

His wife Mary began to notice a change in his behaviour; he began acting out of character. Instead of keeping busy doing various farm chores, he would spend hours sitting in silence by the kitchen window, staring vacantly at distant fields. Occasionally, he would shift his position to ease the pain in his neck. On mail days he would clutch the offensive freight bill in his hand and hurry into the bedroom, silently closing the door behind him. Sometimes he sat on the bed for hours, doing nothing.

About a year later he again experienced a financial disaster. His efforts to raise pigs in quantity had been successful. Many of his pigs weighed within a pound or two of ideal market weight and he decided to sell around forty pigs. Zeb was advised by a neighbour that he would get a better price for his pigs if he shipped them to market by rail rather than by selling them in the local stockyard. Deciding to take the advice of his neighbour, he loaded them into a railway livestock car and shipped them off.

Two days later, the railway company sent him the bad news. The freight charges exceeded the value of his pigs and he now owed two freight bills: one for his oats, and one for his hogs. To add insult to injury, interest charges rapidly increased his debt.

Zeb's behavior continued to deteriorate. He lost all interest in the farm. He could not even be bothered to help milk the cows or take care of the livestock. His wife Mary and the older children now struggled to keep the farm going. Mary became convinced that his mind had become very disturbed.

She was correct in this observation. The combination of physical and mental pain had become too much for him to bear. One mail day, Zeb went into the bedroom carrying not only the railway letters, but this time he also carried his .22 rifle. He wept quietly as he extracted the freight bills and added them to his ever-growing collection.

He then loaded his rifle, placed the end of the gun barrel in his mouth and pulled the trigger.

When Mary rushed into the bedroom, she found him sprawled on the floor in a spreading pool of blood, surrounded by scattered freight bills.

Finally Zeb was at peace with the world.

One Less Status Symbol

I was stricken with scarlet fever in the fall of 1939, when I was fourteen years old. Since this disease was contagious, my father and my sisters were ordered by the doctor to live with relatives while my mother stayed at home to take care of me.

I became very ill. Sixty years later I can still remember the delirium that I suffered. It was like a continuous nightmare or a horror movie.

On the third day of my illness I began to recover. My appetite started to return and I almost felt human again. However, I was still very weak.

Late that night I suddenly woke up with a very jittery feeling of apprehension. When I opened my eyes I realized that my bedroom was no longer in complete darkness. An eerie light from an outside source was flashing through my bedroom window. The light was not constant. It flickered and shimmered as it reflected from my bedroom walls. I shifted closer to the window and looked out. My view was dominated by the Catholic church about three hundred feet away. The church had a fresh coat of white paint, which now gleamed with fast-moving reflections. There were several shades of red ranging from pink to crimson.

It was obvious that the church walls were reflecting the flames of a very big fire. Which building was on fire? Our town was a small community, less than five hundred people, and there were few large buildings. Outside of six grain elevators, the brick school, the churches and the town hall, there were no tall structures.

I was still too weak to walk on my own, so I could not move to another window for a better view. I called to my mother who woke up and rushed to a front window. She could clearly see flames and sparks shooting up in the sky from one of the grain elevators.

Cudworth was ill-prepared to fight a fire. The town had no community water supply. Everyone relied upon private wells for a water supply. There was no fire department. The nearest fire hydrant was in Saskatoon, nearly seventy miles away.

Sixty years ago it was common for teenagers to rate a prairie community on the basis of the number of grain elevators. These magnificent structures, so clearly visible on the prairie landscape, were the ultimate status symbol. In the eyes of the young folk, the number of grain elevators clearly reflected the importance of a community in terms of both economic well-being and culture. A one-elevator town was definitely at the low end of the scale, and provided the grounds for a pejorative comment. A two-elevator town was more than twice as important, and so on as the count of elevators increased.

Our elevator was entirely consumed by the fire that night. A couple of days passed before the ashes cooled down. As soon as this occurred, "needy" farmers and their families appeared on the scene equipped with large pails. They methodically searched through the ashes gathering nails and spikes for use on the farm.

Someone commented that the laminated construction of each elevator necessitated the use of several tons of nails.

Anyway, the results of the fire were not all negative. I am sure that no one today could be bothered to do a salvage job like that. One has to remember that during the 30's there were many desperate people in our country.

The burnt-out elevator at Cudworth was not replaced and its absence posed a negative impact on our community "bragging rights".

Outhouse Memories

I never heard the sound of a flushing toilet until I was fourteen years old. It was on the occasion of my first visit to Saskatoon in 1939 to see the King and Queen. At the time it seemed as though there was a regal relationship because the toilet was referred to as the "throne".

Outhouses were the predominant back yard feature in our little town (Cudworth, Sask.).

If I sat in the corner chair in our kitchen and craned my neck a bit to one side or another while looking out the window, it was possible to see at least seven outhouses in one panoramic inspection.

To the north there were two matching outhouses about fifty feet apart and the same distance behind the church. These were undoubtedly the best cared-for sanitary (?) facilities in the town. They were grey with white trim, and were re-painted every two or three years. Across the back alley I could see three more, weather beaten and battered with no evidence of ever having been painted. By cocking my head a bit to the left I could catch a glimpse of the Doctor's stately, newly-painted two-holer across the street. Our own comfort station looked weathered and old in contrast to its brand-new galvanized hinges. It took up a friendly position beside our garage. In our neighbour's yard to the south stood a forlorn, slightly leaning structure whose boards on one side were riddled with large embarrassing knot holes.

Yes, there were out-door privies everywhere. Small wonder that I did not realize that there actually were more sanitary and comfortable toilets in existence. During the Depression very few Cudworth households had the where-with-all to buy toilet paper. I doubt whether most small-town general merchants even kept a stock of toilet paper to sell. Obviously, alternatives were used. Even those who could afford to buy the product stayed with long established traditions employing the use of newspaper and/or the Eaton's catalogue.

The pages of the Eaton's catalogue were too glossy to be rated as a first class wipe. However, they were superior to the printer's ink that was emitted from the newspaper. The catalogue was in wide use because it had many pages and was free. When crumpled and wrinkled, it served the purpose. In addition to providing an essential service, the catalogue also provided an opportunity for intellectual stimulation. While waiting for things to happen, the outhouse occupant could become a "browser" who made many theoretical shopping decisions. As a lad my main focus was directed at the toy section which displayed items my parents simply could not afford to buy. (One Christmas I got only a handkerchief and a mandarin orange.)

As autumn approached, the Eaton's catalogue had shed most of its pages, and anxious eyes looked westward for a change. The fruit of the Okanagan was highly rated by prairie people, who spared no effort to save enough money to by B.C. fruit. Peaches were generally rated as number one, not only for their mouth-watering flavor, but also for their wrappings. Each peach was carefully wrapped in a big square of tissue paper. This paper was aromatic, soft to the touch and had a high absorbency - ideal attributes for outhouse use.

Just before Christmas an extra bonus was in store for families not in the "needy" class. The train would discharge a big shipment of Japanese oranges for the festive season. The fruit was packaged in small wooden boxes, and each delicious orange was wrapped in tissue paper. This substantially extended the comfort zone if a family could afford to buy several boxes.

In addition to providing an essential sanitary service, outhouses often became a target once a year, at Halloween. For mischievous teen-aged boys it had become a challenge to tip over at least a few outhouses after dark on Halloween. This activity may have provided an enjoyable adventure for young lads, but for the homeowner it could be a disaster. Ancient rickety outhouses sometimes collapsed entirely during tipping. Usually some degree of structural damage occurred.

October 1942 was the one and only time that I participated in this Halloween prank. In order to discourage any mischievous antics of the high school students, our school principal, Otto Lang, organized a high school Halloween party at school. During the festivities, six of us boys quietly left the school party, ran to the principal's home two blocks away from school, lifted his toilet and carefully transported it to the school yard where we deposited it near the front door of the school. What a party!

The next day at school we expected more than just a reprimand. To our surprise our principal, with a twinkle in his eye, asked if the perpetrators would kindly return his toilet to its proper home site. Not an angry word was spoken, and we returned the outhouse immediately.

After the school party had ended, our little group of teenagers still sought adventure and excitement so we tipped a few toilets. We were very careful to avoid damage. The proprietor of the beer store, Jack Eul, owned a very large outhouse in which he stored his storm windows. When we tipped it, we took special care, and gently lowered it to the ground without breaking a single pane of glass.

I also discovered that by joining this group of toilet tippers, I had insured that my parent's privy would not be disturbed.

I still have clear but very unpleasant memories of some outhouses. The big four-room brick school, which housed grades five to twelve, was serviced by two huge outdoor toilets. The girls' toilet was located at the south boundary of the school yard and boys' at the north boundary. I never checked out the girls' facility. I can speak only of the boys'. It consisted of a building divided into six stalls. An uncovered space outside of the building was enclosed by a tall wooden fence for privacy. It was equipped with a sloping tin-clad trough leading to a trench under the building. It was a primitive and disgusting structure, both in winter and in summer.

Once winter had set in, the temperature would remain below freezing for many months. In early winter, the urine would run to the bottom of the trough before freezing. As winter progressed the yellow ice would increase in both depth and length, until eventually the entire trough would be covered by a thick sheet of ice.

The warm conditions of early spring promoted a spring thaw, and eventually "spring break-up" of the ice in the trough. This transformation was soon followed by the summer heat. The entire facility soon reeked of a horrible stench and was used only in a dire emergency.

During all the years that I attended this school, I never witnessed a teacher entering or leaving these outdoor facilities. Eventually, I became convinced that all school teachers were equipped with extraordinary plumbing systems.

Bitter Harvest

In the 1930's, Debden was a small village of about sixty souls, situated sixty miles northwest of Prince Albert, Saskatchewan. Like hundreds of other prairie communities, the citizens of Debden and the surrounding farms helped each other out during the Depression, and worked together to face a common enemy - poverty.

My friend George Chalifour who was raised on a farm near Debden recalls a glaring exception to this unwritten code of conduct. His memory of this incident is very sharp, since it nearly tore his family apart.

George's parents had been married sixteen years when this event took place. They had always enjoyed mutual respect and understanding and together had created a family atmosphere where both children and parents felt comfortable with one another. Despite hard times and a shortage of what is today considered essential to family enjoyment, they were satisfied with their lot. Suddenly, a deep rift opened up between the parents and threatened this fine example of family harmony.

The trouble started in the fall of 1935 during the harvest season. Frequent rain showers in late July and August delayed the harvest for several weeks. Amedi Chalifour (George's father) owned a threshing outfit, and it was used to harvest his neighbor's crops as well as his own. Finally, the threshing operation got underway in early September. The weather stayed dry and sunny and harvesting progressed rapidly. They finished threshing at all the neighbors, and action was scheduled to begin at the Chalifour farm the next day.

However, there was a sudden turn of events which caused a delay. A neighboring farmer, John Worth (not his real name) , who had never hired the Chalifour threshing operation, stood out in the road and intercepted each hay rack as it appeared. He instructed the threshing crew to enter his fields and load up. When Amedi finally arrived with the threshing outfit, he was quite surprised. But he was just too nice a guy to insist that the operation should first start on his own farm. Threshing on the Worth farm was completed in less than a week, and the outfit then moved to the Chalifour farm.

The weather changed over night. A gentle rain was falling when the crew woke up. The rainfall picked up the pace by noon, and later in the day turned into a steady downpour. The crew members dispersed to their own farms.

The next day was much the same, except the temperature started to drop. That night a freezing rain occurred,coating the stooks with over an inch of ice. Precipitation ceased but the weather remained cold. Amedi became optimistic that he could soon begin threshing. His hopes vanished when he discovered that the stooks were frozen to the ground. With an axe he chopped a few stooks free only to find that the bundles were sopping wet inside.

A week later the temperature rose well above freezing and the wet grain began to germinate. Soon every stook displayed a crown of newly sprouted green shoots. Over the winter the remaining grain kernels were harvested by mice, geese and elk.

The loss of their crop had serious consequences for the Chalifour family. There was no money available for extras at Christmas, and toward the end of the winter they could not afford to buy kerosene for the lamps. Up at daylight; to bed at dusk.

To add insult to injury John Worth did not show up to pay the money owed for threshing his grain. Amedi was not an aggressive person, so he did not try to collect. On the other hand, his wife Dolly was finding it more and more difficult to manage the household with inadequate funds. So she decided to go after the money herself.

One morning she walked over to the Worth farm and asked for the money. She was stunned by John's reply. He said, "I paid your husband cash two months ago. If he didn't give any to you, perhaps he lost it at the poker table in town." His wife confirmed her husband's statement. She told Dolly that she had seen her husband pay Amedi with cash. The two of them sounded so convincing that Dolly believed them. When she returned home she accused Amedi of lying to her and they got into a terrible argument. Over the next few months they had frequent arguments, and even discussed separation. Somehow they healed their wounds and re-established their good relationship. George remembers those days. All of the children were fearful that the family would be broken up.

After nearly forty years on the farm the Chalifour's sold out in 1958. To begin with, they operated a cafe business in Debden for a couple of years. In 1960 they sold that business, and prepared to move to Port Alberni, B.C. to join their son George. All of their household goods were packed and dispatched in a moving van. Amedi and Dolly had packed their bags and were saying good byes to some friends when a car drove up. To their surprise, John Worth and his wife had come to see them. But their visit was not only to say good bye.

John reached into his pocket and pulled out four fifty dollar bills. He said, "I've come here today to admit that I lied about me paying you for the threshing you did twenty-five years ago. For some time now my conscience has been bothering me so much that I can't get a decent night's sleep any more. Here is two hundred dollars which covers what I owe you for the threshing bill."

Amedi replied, "Actually the bill was only one hundred eighty-two dollars and seventy-five cents. I'll never forget that amount because we were so poor that winter that we needed every single penny. However, I am not prepared to accept your offer. I'll feel quite content knowing that your sleepless nights will continue. You nearly ruined the lives of an entire family: father, mother and six children by your dishonesty. And I cannot forget. You witnessed the loss of my entire wheat crop in 1935 and you did not lift a finger to help us in our need. And I cannot forget that either. I don't want your money. I don't need your money."

Amedi and Dolly climbed into their car and left Debden for a new life in B.C., very conscious of the strong bonds that had held them together through thick and thin.

Wheels of Fortune

This anecdote originated on a farm near Debden, Saskatchewan, as told by George Chalifour now living in Victoria.

My brothers and I could hardly recall riding in our Dad's old Model T Ford. Ever since 1929, this old car had been parked on blocks in the bush behind the barn, sort of rotting away under full exposure to the elements. Our family simply could not afford to operate it.

In 1938 my brothers and I decided that we would like to revive this old crate. The tires were not in bad shape. We had to pump air into them. It needed oil so we got some used crankcase oil that had been in the tractor. We filled the fuel tank with purple gas. My older brother, who had a fair amount of mechanical knowledge, discovered that the coil would no longer function so he got one from the blacksmith. With a bit of monkey wrenching, we managed to get the engine going and we were soon on the road: no licence, no insurance, illegal tax-free fuel and completely inexperienced drivers.

We seldom saw a Mountie in these parts - maybe once in two or three years. So despite our limitations, we did not hesitate to drive on the local dirt roads. There were no highways or we probably would have gone there too.

To our surprise we were stopped by a Mountie. Evidently there had been some stealing going on and he was investigating. He checked us out, gave us a lecture on the laws of operating a motor vehicle, and sent us home. We didn't let his advice bother us too long, because we again drove out into the country the next weekend. Wouldn't you know it! The same Mountie stopped us and escorted us home where he had a discussion with Dad about breaking the law. We were forbidden to drive.

The next time that our family had a "car experience" involved our Mom. Were we surprised! Every once in a while our Mom would take time out to enter contests that were advertised in the local store. She had spent over an hour to compose a couple of paragraphs for a laundry soap called CHIPSO. She completed the statement, "I like CHIPSO because..." In putting her submission together, she focused on two main ingredients: a generous input of homespun humor, as well as lashings of down-to-earth common sense which she had accumulated during twenty years of rural life on an economically marginal farm.

It was in September that she got a registered letter informing her that of all the thousands of entries from the U.S.A. and Canada, she had won first prize. This certainly brightened up her day. The prize consisted of a brand new 1938 Chevrolet De Luxe sedan worth around $2500.00; two thousand gallons of gas; plus all hotel and meal expenses for a two-week holiday anywhere in the U.S.A. and Canada.

She could hardly wait to tell Dad. He had been in the Prince Albert hospital for over a month. He had serious lung problems stemming from exposure to chlorine gas in WW1. The previous year the doctor had given him six months to live. It was the third time that he had been hospitalized this year, and the expenses of specialists and hospital care were growing rapidly.

Mom traveled by train to Prince Albert to visit Dad. After he heard the news about her prize, they started to dream of a holiday to Yellowstone Park and the Grand Canyon. But after a few minutes of reverie they became silent as reality replaced dreams. They both realized that they were deeply in debt, mostly because of medical bills. She composed a letter to the contest manager explaining their circumstances. In reply she received a cheque for the full value of the car and the gasoline. They could not be reimbursed for the holiday expenses, since they would not be incurred.

After a few years, my parents moved to B.C. My dad's health suddenly improved and he managed to enjoy life until he died at the age of seventy-nine.

A Fifteen Cent Paring Knife

*Here is a Depression era story told by Bud Bondesen, another senior curler in Victoria. He describes his life in Calgary where his unemployed father struggled to support his family.**

Living in a house crammed with people never struck me as being strange, or abnormal, or even just a bit unusual. It was probably because I did not know any better.

Until my dad died suddenly in 1937, there were eleven of us, two entire families, jointly occupying living quarters designed to accommodate a family of four people.

You might ask, "How come so many people lived in such a small house? Why was it necessary for two families to crowd themselves into such a small space?"

The answer is quite simple. My father and his friend, Frank Hawes, became unemployed almost immediately after the stock market collapse of 1929. They both had good jobs working in a smelter in Calgary. The smelter closed its doors in 1929, and did not resume production until the war started in 1939.

City relief assistance was minimal, so Dad and Frank decided to share living quarters to reduce the cost of rent, heating and elec-

*For additional details read the anecdote HARD-NOSED BUD.

tricity. Our two families pooled their resources. We ate all our meals together. As one big family, we went on outings beyond city limits to pick saskatoon berries and chokecherries, and, jointly, took care of a large vegetable garden

During those years of co-habitation, all of us children shared one huge upstairs bedroom. Three Bondesen children and four Hawes children slept on mattresses laid out, wall-to-wall, on the floor.

I always felt that I had a pretty normal childhood. I cannot recall feeling sorry for myself for being deprived of many things that other kids took for granted; most of the kids I knew were no better off than I was. I don't recall being unhappy for more than a few minutes. There were no unfulfilled expectations. No unkept promises. I had friends who enjoyed the same fun and games that I did. Only much later, as I entered my teens, did it dawn on me that our family was close to impoverishment, and that I would have to strive very hard to make a living.

I must admit that there was one aspect of my childhood that really bugged me. To this day, I confess that I truly hate and detest oatmeal porridge. I remember so clearly that in real tough times when the cupboard was bare, we had porridge three times a day for what seemed like weeks.

In the morning my mom would cook a huge pot of oatmeal porridge. We would eat only a small part for breakfast, usually with no sugar or milk. I do recall that Saskatoon berry preserves would sometimes be added to dress it up. At lunch time, if there was bread available, some of the left-over porridge was used to make sandwiches, garnished with jam if available. For supper the remaining porridge was fried. None of us kids enjoyed this food

(?), but we knew that if it was not eaten it would reappear on our plates at the next meal. I suppose my dislike for porridge at age seventy could be called a phobia. I prefer to call it a Depression hangover.

It was around 1936 or 1937 that an event occurred which gave me an insight into my dad's character. Dad had not had work for a long time, probably over a month. One day, out of the clear blue, opportunity literally came knocking at our door. An old friend appeared at our home and asked Dad if he would like to work the next day emptying a box car of coal that had arrived from Drumheller. Of course, my dad jumped at the chance.

The next morning I got out of bed when I heard Dad getting ready to go to work. He was about to leave when he remembered that he had not made a lunch. In checking out the cupboard he found only a quarter loaf of bread. He looked at it for a couple of seconds, left it for the family, shrugged his shoulders, tucked his empty lunch bucket under his arm and left for work. He took the lunch bucket so that his fellow workers would not know that he had not packed a bite to eat. Three men emptied that coal car that day. When noon came, no one wanted to stop for lunch. As the day wore on, it became obvious that three empty lunch buckets stood side by side.

* * *

When dad was lucky enough to get a day's work he would sometimes stop at a butcher shop on the way home and buy a big piece of flank steak for fifteen or twenty cents. Mom would tenderize the meat by beating it with a special wooden mallet, stuff it with the same kind of dressing she used for chicken, roll it up tight, tie it with a cord and bake this "mock duck" in the oven. That night the Hawes and Bondesens would dine in style, a real feast.

There were even a few times that our menu took on a gourmet character. This occurred during the summer after a day or two of heavy rain. My dad would check out the stock yards down by the railroad tracks, about a half mile from our home. The rain would sometimes cause the sprouting of thousands of mushrooms from the manure covered pens, and Dad could easily pick two five-gallon pails of mushrooms in a morning.

We ate these freshly cooked delicacies for a day or two, but Mom canned most of them for later use. We may not have dined like royalty, but we didn't have short rations all the time, either.

* * *

I also have clear memories about one special Christmas dinner. Many years later, I learned that the entree would properly have been called "roast squab". It all started when my dad and Mr. Hawes checked out the idle, shut-down smelter where they had worked. The huge steel buildings were rusting and silent and empty. However, these relics of a busy time now provided an attractive roosting site for hundreds of pigeons. These birds roosted high up among the rafters and beams. The only sounds in this once bustling place were the cooing and feather-rustling of the pigeons. Home-made chicken-wire cages were placed strategically on the beams. Dad and Frank trapped over a dozen birds for our Christmas dinner. The two ladies of the house worked hard to prepare the pigeons which completely filled a large roasting pan. I'm sure it was our tastiest meal of the entire Depression.

* * *

The events associated with our 1936 Christmas are well preserved in my memory. My parents always tried hard to provide something special for Christmas, but they were nearly flat broke that year.

On December twenty-fourth, after our bowl of porridge, my dad announced to us children that he would take us Christmas shopping. We wore our warmest clothes and walked to the street serviced by streetcars. I was nine years old and my two sisters were seven and five. The streetcar fare was five cents for kids and ten cents for adults. Dad could not afford to ride the street car so he walked the two and a half miles to the Hudson's Bay store. He asked me to take care of my little sisters on the streetcar and be sure to get off at the right place. I felt very proud to be given this responsibility.

The three of us soon arrived at the Bay. I made sure that we got off at the right place. We were warmly dressed, and didn't mind standing outside in the cold waiting for Dad.

We stood in front of a huge display window, brightly lit, and featuring many toys. My sisters were mostly interested in the dolls. I was fascinated by an electric train that ran on a huge circular track, through tunnels and over trestles.

When Dad showed up, he dug his hand in his pocket and pulled out some loose change. It was all the money that he had. He gave a quarter to each child to buy Christmas gifts. He then returned fifteen cents to his pocket for our return street car fare. All that remained in his hand were three nickels.

I no longer remember the gifts that I bought with my quarter, mostly candy, I think. However, I still recall Dad's purchase of a gift for Mom.

I watched him as he quietly walked from one table display to another. First, he looked at some ladies' things. He closely examined an elegant boudoir set. There was a mirror, a hair brush, and a long-handled comb. He did not examine the set for long.

Mom would have been delighted with such a gift. Dad gave the set one last look, shook his head slowly, and walked to a table displaying kitchen things. Most of the utensils cost much more than he could afford. He looked through the heap of things for several minutes, and finally selected one item that cost exactly fifteen cents. It was a wooden-handled paring knife. It would have to do.

For me the day had been an exciting and rewarding experience. I did not focus on negative aspects, like dad having to walk five miles. Instead I felt warmly toward my dad for trusting me to look after my little sisters.

* * *

In 1936, we could not afford to buy a Christmas tree, even though an average tree cost only thirty-five cents. Dad and Frank Hawes held a "council of war" and became determined to get a Christmas tree for the two families by hook or by crook.

The Pierce estate was located near the eastern outskirts of Calgary. It was about twenty acres in size and beautifully landscaped with all sorts of deciduous and evergreen trees. Although it was over three miles from our house, dad and Frank walked there after dark, cut a six-foot spruce tree and carried it all the way home. For decorations, the mothers and the older girls of our extended family prepared popcorn strings, colourful paper chains and silver paper stars. Some candle holders were clipped onto the branches and the candles were lit for a few minutes during our Christmas dinner. Mom was very artistic so she made eleven neat little baskets of different coloured strips of paper, while Mrs. Hawes made a big batch of fudge. Each basket was filled with delicious cubes of fudge, so everyone had at least one Christmas present.

I cannot remember many gifts beyond the candy baskets. However, I clearly recall my mother's response when she received the little paring knife. After opening the gift, she whispered a very quiet "Thank you, dear" in a rather squeaky voice. There were tears of joy in her eyes as she pecked Dad on the cheek. From the expression on her face you'd have thought she had just received a diamond necklace. Dad gave her a little hug, and quietly smiled.

* * *

The Depression shattered many lives. But because of my dad and his great love for his family, none of us grew up deeply scarred by tough times. My major regret is that my dad did not live to see the end of the Depression. He missed out entirely on Canada's return to more prosperous times.

He was such a kind and generous person. Although it happened over sixty years ago, I still remember the look on Dad's face while he selected that fifteen cent paring knife, giving all he had, and wishing it could be so much more.

Hard-Nosed Bud

The members of the Victoria Senior Men's Curling Club have much in common. Of course age is the most obvious. Most of us are in our seventies and eighties. A close second commonality is the nature of our tonsorial features. There is a predominance of white and grey hair as well as a generous representation of varying degrees of baldness. Our immigrant status is another common feature of the group as only a handful of members were born and raised in Victoria. The majority of the "migrants" came from the prairie provinces, with Saskatchewan well in the lead.

By far the majority of our members have taken up permanent residence in Victoria; however, there are still a few stalwarts who maintain homes east of the Rockies. They enjoy the prairie winter until the New Year when they migrate to Victoria to enjoy the last half of the curling season.

Usually the members of each curling team will drink coffee together immediately following a game. We will discuss many subjects. These will vary from comments on sports to off-colour jokes or current events, but eventually the conversation will focus some attention to health issues. At our age this is indeed a vital subject. We discuss those curlers who have just gone into the hospital as well as those who have just come out. We also fondly remember those who didn't make it. With an air of hope in our voices, we discuss the merits of overcoming worn-out knees by delivering our rocks from a standing position with the help of a special delivery stick. Sometimes a round table tally is made of those who have not yet experienced serious prostate problems. Occasional reference is made to the effectiveness of Viagra, but the subject seldom arouses much interest.

Another popular subject among the senior curling fraternity involves the Health Care System. One of the most tragic stories originated from my friend Bud Bondesen, who clearly recalls the inequalities of health care during the Depression. If you didn't have the money, you could not get medical care unless, of course, a doctor would work for nothing, or was willing to barter his services for farm produce.

Bud was born in 1927 on a farm near Lockport, Manitoba, a few miles from Winnipeg. A year later his family moved to Calgary where his father had been offered a good job with Dominion Rolling Mills. This firm bought scrap metal and produced such items as ingots, rods, and angle iron. Unfortunately, in 1929 the operation was shut down completely, and did not resume work until war broke out in September of 1939.

Bud's father had periodically suffered from a stomach ulcer problem, and this malady flared up with a vengeance during the Depression. Unfortunately he could not afford appropriate medical treatment. Finally in 1937, at the age of thirty-two, he was taken to the hospital in an emergency situation. A few hours later he died on the operating room table.

As an eight-year-old boy, Bud also experienced a medical problem but it was not as disastrous as his father's. He suffered a most unusual accident. One day a friend had come over before lunch to play. They had a great time all afternoon. Just before supper his friend boarded a streetcar to return home. As the streetcar departed, Bud ran parallel on the sidewalk and used a pea shooter to try to hit his friend through an open window of the streetcar. In a few seconds the streetcar accelerated rapidly and Bud had to run full tilt in order to continue his little game. He faced the streetcar as he ran and didn't see a telephone pole until a split second before impact. The pole smashed his nose and knocked him unconscious.

When he came to, his face was a terrible mess. Fortunately, only his nose suffered severe damage. Bud was taken to the hospital and a minor repair job was done to stop the bleeding. Since this accident occurred in the midst of the Depression, the family had no money for reconstructive surgery. Bud soon recovered from the accident, but emerged with a nose that looked like it belonged to a retired pugilist.

In 1939 at age twelve, Bud followed in his father's foot steps by getting a part-time job at the Dominion Rolling Mill. The plant had just resumed production with the advent of the second world war. In order to help his family financially, Bud left school after completing grade nine and took full-time employment .

In 1944 Bud and his buddy decided to go to B.C. and seek employment in the forest industry. According to rumour, the pay was twice what he earned in the mill in Calgary. They could not afford to pay for transportation so they hopped a freight train. They carried only a bottle of water; and had no food, no extra clothing, and no money. No one had told them about the Connaught tunnel and they were both frightened and filthy with soot when the train emerged.

Upon their arrival in Vancouver, they were both immediately hired by A.P.L. (Alberni Pacific Limited) . Bud was hired as a chokerman and his buddy got the job of whistle punk. They were paid around ninety cents an hour, and worked in a logging camp near Port Alberni on Vancouver Island. When Bud turned eighteen he traveled to Victoria and joined the Navy.

After basic training he became a member of the "black gang" in the engine room. He stayed with the Navy for nine years until a severe lung disorder developed from the engine room environment. Bud was discharged for medical reasons and awarded a small disability pension.

One of the most substantive benefits that Bud obtained from his military service concerned the Navy's medical proficiency. Very soon after he joined the service, his badly disfigured nose was closely examined by medical staff. He was given the opportunity for reconstructive surgery which would restore his nose to its proper shape. This time there would be no medical fee. Bud readily accepted the offer.

While under an anaesthetic, his nose was smashed and all of the bone fragments were removed by a suction device. A piece of bone was removed from his hip and grafted to form his newly constituted "shnozzle". This solid bone nose is now as hard as a hammer.

The tough times during the Depression had been a character-building experience for Bud, which he later put to good use after his discharge from the Navy in 1945. Despite having only a grade nine school certificate, Bud undertook his own study program. While working for the Department of National Defense, he advanced steadily as a stationary engineer, and eventually was promoted to Chief Engineer at H.M.C.S. Naden in Victoria.

Bud still has vibrant memories of the inequality of the Canadian health care system (or lack of it) which prevailed during the Depression. The early death of his father could probably have been prevented by timely surgery if he could have afforded to pay for it. The lack of adequate treatment after his own accident also caused him both physical and mental pain. When someone mentions the need for a two-tiered system in this country, Bud thinks of the many tears shed over the system in vogue during his youth.

You Can't Eat Lumber

Some Canadians are well aware of the generous support given to Canadian war veterans by the Federal Government following World War II. Perhaps the greatest expression of national gratitude was the monetary aid given through DVA (Department of Veteran's Affairs) toward providing university education. Thousands of veterans also took advantage of the Veteran's Land Act (VLA) to obtain a home and sizeable plot of land at minimum cost. Veterans not able to use these benefits were given gratuities, the amount of cash based on length of military service. Moreover, long after the war, DVA has continued to help veterans when needed. No doubt about it. Canada's record of helping ex-servicemen compares most favourably with any other country.

To a certain degree this comprehensive level of support may have evolved from action taken after World War I. At that time the SSB (Soldier's Settlement Board) was created to help veterans obtain a farm and become self-supporting. Emphasis was placed upon settling the prairie provinces, where there still was considerable unoccupied land, but land was also made available elsewhere in Canada, e.g. Black Creek on Vancouver Island.

John Silver (not his real name) was an Englishman who joined the British Navy in 1901 at age twenty-one. He became a petty officer and served as a fourth class steam engineer on a variety of ships for twenty-two years. During the first world war, his ship was torpedoed in the Battle of Jutland, and he was one of the few survivors. He was discharged from the Navy in 1923. During the next two years he tried several ways of making a living. For a while he was a shop owner, but he was too soft-hearted to become a successful business man. He allowed customers too much credit, and went broke. Eventually he and his brother-in-law sought information about settling in Canada. They discovered that the SSB would help British ex-servicemen get a start in farming .

In 1925 the brothers arrived with their families in Alberta, and started to put down their roots. John borrowed $5200 at 6% interest from the SSB to purchase a farm plus livestock, machinery, building materials and other paraphernalia. An annual payment of around $300.00 was payable at harvest time. The SSB maintained a staff of inspectors who provided advice to the farmers and insured that the loan was indeed secure.

John had maintained membership in the Naval Reserve, so in 1926 he spent two weeks on a refresher course at the Esquimalt Naval Station. Upon his return to his Alberta farm it was apparent that he enjoyed Navy life much more than farming.

During the Depression the combination of poor commodity prices and poor crops became overwhelming, and by 1935 John was unable to make his annual loan payment. He did not even have enough money to purchase seed grain to put in a crop. When he appealed to the SSB for help, it was suggested that he cease farming and rent the farm to someone else, which he did. He was allowed to continue living on the farm and to maintain a few cows, some chickens and turkeys and a big vegetable garden.

As the Depression continued, John was constantly on the lookout for a job. At one point in time, because he was a qualified stationary engineer, he was offered a job to operate a power plant in a sawmill. He was about to start work when he discovered that he would not be paid wages. Instead, he would have to accept lumber in lieu of wages. When he informed his wife, she commiserated and said, "We can't eat lumber!" In the end, he could not accept the job although he was desperate for work.

All of the forgoing information was provided to me by John's youngest son Peter, who was six years old when the family settled in Alberta. By the time he became a teenager, Peter was closely attached to the land and to farming generally. He wanted to have a farm of his own but due to necessity he took a job as a cowboy and stayed with it for two years. He learned how to brand and round-up cattle, break horses and care for sick or injured animals. He liked the work but found that there was little Hollywood glamour in the job, especially when riding herd in the rain and wind on a wet horse.

His talent as a hard-working, capable young man did not go unnoticed. He was hired by a prominent agriculturist to take charge of a 640-acre farm. Peter was only seventeen years old. This farm was a complex operation involving the culture of a variety of crops: one thousand lambs, fifty hogs, one hundred steers, many horses as well as one hundred fifty silver foxes. In his spare time Peter would "break" young horses. His salary was twenty-five dollars per month plus free room and board. (At that time a hired man on a prairie farm was paid five dollars per month outside of the harvest season).

Peter's brother had joined the Canadian Navy in 1931. In the winter of 1939, Peter traveled to Victoria to visit him. He took advantage of an excursion rate of fifteen dollars to travel via the CPR from Calgary to Vancouver . Peter fell in love with Victoria and he also admired his brother's life in the Navy. He was also attracted to the army, and joined the Canadian Scottish Regiment. In 1940 the regiment was posted to Nova Scotia for a year's training. The soldiers trained for winter warfare, with skis and with full pack. They were then issued tropical gear (short pants and puttees). They were rather confused and didn't know whether they would end up in North Africa or Sweden.

Soon after he arrived in England in early 1942, Peter received distressing news from home. His father had died. Shortly after, Peter was informed that an SSB representative had visited his father in the cancer clinic and persuaded him to sign a quit claim deed for the farm, while he was under heavy sedation. His mother's name was not on the land title, so upon her husband's death she lost the farm. A few months later the old family home on the farm burned down and she lost everything.

Peter's unit took part in the Normandy invasion. He and two buddies came under sniper fire. His buddies were killed but Peter survived with a severe wound in his arm.

Peter, who has just entered his eighties, occasionally becomes a little nostalgic. He is grateful for having had the opportunity to take on a heavy load of responsibility while still a teenager. These experiences seem to have provided a great deal of stability to his life. Here are a few of his memories of Depression days.

When Peter entered his teens he had a keen interest in baseball. He inherited a glove from an older brother, but there was no uniform available. After he told his mother that all the other players had uniforms, she decided to take action. She bleached several flour sacks, cut out a pattern and turned out a respectable uniform in a couple of hours. She cut out the letters of his name in black cloth and sewed them across the shoulders. He was the envy of every kid on the team.

When Peter reached the age of fifteen he discovered that some of his friends had sneaked into the local beer parlor on a Saturday night and enjoyed a few glasses of forbidden froth with older brothers. Peter decided to give it a try. He prepared for the event by avoiding hair cuts and not shaving for several weeks. After a pale fuzzy beard appeared on his chin he decided to give it a try. However, the beard was hardly visible so he combed in some black shoe polish. His first attempt to joins his friends in the beer parlor proved to be successful. Having succeeded, he no longer felt the challenge and did not get into the habit of beer drinking.

In 1936 he worked on a nearby farm during the harvest season. After laboring hard at stooking and pitching bundles for a month, the job was completed. At that time his boss informed him that he had no money for wages. He offered to give Peter a 1928 Chevrolet sedan in lieu of wages. However, the car was worth more than the wages owed, so to complete the deal , Peter gave him a couple of pigs.

A few years later when Peter was in the army, the farmer took possession of the car, claiming that Peter still owed something on the deal.

I guess if there is a message in this story it would go something like this. Sometimes it takes more than poor commodity prices and crop failures to force farmers to leave their farms. In this case it was the SSM bureaucracy which triggered the event.

Peter retired after a successful career in the British Columbia Forest Service, and was able to afford the luxury of reliving a boyhood dream. He bought a saddle horse which he keeps on a farm a few miles from his home. Once a week he goes for a ride, bringing back pleasant memories of an Alberta ranch over sixty years ago.

Hardscrabble Farm

A few wisps of dust trailed faintly behind a tanker wagon lumbering along a narrow country road. The rig was being hauled by four horses. The only sound was a low-pitched creaking noise from the wooden-spoked wheels as they churned up the dust.

The horses were a pitiful-looking foursome. They looked sad and scrawny and displayed no spirit. The shapes of their backbones and rib cages were clearly distinguishable beneath their shabby hides. There was not an ounce of fat on them.

The harness was nearly completely worn out. It was barely serviceable. The horse collars were battered, and the stuffing protruded from gaping holes. Haywire had been substituted to replace worn out or broken leather straps.

The driver was only thirteen years old. His name was Walter Fink, and he was driving the tanker wagon three miles to fetch 500 gallons of fresh water from a farmer's well.

Walter's general appearance more or less matched the look of his horses. He was very thin. Since he wore no shoes and socks all summer, the soles of his feet were as tough as shoe leather. He wore faded bib overalls which had many multicolored patches. The knees and the seat had been recently worn through and could use another repair job. The sleeves of his faded shirt hung in tatters. A stained and misshapen straw hat completed his attire.

Usually, two members of his family would make this water trip, because filling the tank was a laborious task. It involved pumping the water by hand into a bucket and then handing the filled bucket to someone perched on a wagon wheel, who would then dump the water into the wooden tank. It was going to take him ages to fill the tank without help.

As the horses plodded tediously down the road, Walter let his eyes wander slowly over the landscape. A broad panoramic view stretched out before him, but offered nothing beautiful or inspiring. It was a defeated landscape. The fields within sight of the road were a prelude to poverty. The crops were only a few inches tall although it was mid-July. They were already dried out. He could not detect a tinge of green anywhere; not even in the hollows.

In some exposures, piles of dead, windblown tumbleweed and Russian thistle had accumulated along the fences. They presented a partial barrier to the wind, which triggered the deposition of dust from adjacent fields. In some places the dust had formed a deep drift, and the fence posts protruded only a few inches from these "dust dunes".

Walter slowly shifted his thoughts to the harsh reality that his family had faced ever since he could remember. His father Harry had always been a deeply-rooted optimist. Years ago, he had dreamed of owning his own farm, but had not been able to fulfill this dream until he came to Canada. This was during the 1920's when Harry was a share cropper in North Dakota.

In 1928, Harry heard that land was still available for homesteading in Canada. After obtaining more detailed information, he and his family traveled to the Eston area, southwest of Saskatoon. The most productive land had already been claimed by earlier settlers, so Harry was stuck with second-rate land. Initially, he did not place much importance on this fact, because for the first time in his life he enjoyed the pride of ownership.

The farm had many shortcomings, all of which contributed to his ultimate failure. To begin with, he rented a house several miles from his homestead. This necessitated an excessive amount of travel. The farm house was also remote from conveniences: three miles from the nearest school and ten miles from Eston, the nearest community. But the most severe handicap was the complete lack of water supply. At first he thought that he might dig a well, but he found out that previous tenants had hired water dowsers and then dug only dry holes. Harry Fink had to settle for hauling water from three miles away. In very dry summers he had to haul water twice that distance.

These memories flashed through Walter's mind as the wagon slowly moved on its course. Recently, he had heard his father complain about their hardscrabble farm. Walter had immediately understood the exact meaning of this term. He already had recognized that there were many facets contributing to the definition of their hardscrabble farm, each one ultimately ending in disaster or failure. These included: hail storms, dust storms, drought, hard work for little if any return, grasshoppers, late spring frosts, early autumn frosts, an impoverished household, an inadequate water supply, and insufficient and often substandard food for the livestock. He also recognized that a hardscrabble farm was a place of failing hope and growing despair.

Would his father be willing and able to continue cultivating these unyielding acres much longer?

Walter had become completely absorbed by his thoughts, and had taken little notice of his whereabouts. Out of habit, with no command from their driver, the horses turned off the road into Mike Coomb's yard. They stopped on their own at the precise place where the water tank would be filled.

Walter immediately returned to reality and climbed down from the rig. He saw Mike approaching from the house. After quietly greeting Walter, Mike made a suggestion.

"Walter, I see that you're all alone today. You could probably use some help filling your tank. I'll be happy to give you a hand if you accompany me to town. I'm planning to drive into Lancer and pick up supplies for a barn dance next weekend. I could use some company during the trip as well as help in loading up my pickup truck."

Walter welcomed the proposition. Any diversion from his boring routine was high on his wish list. Lancer was situated across the Saskatchewan River. They would have to cross on a ferry. As he and Mike shared a strong interest in sports, the trip would be an enjoyable experience.

They decided to fill the water tank before leaving. Walter unharnessed the horses, watered them, took them to the barn, and fed them some hay. He joined Mike at the well, and they worked together dumping pails of water into the tank.

They were soon on their way to Lancer in the pickup. They crossed the Saskatchewan River on a ferry, and then drove a few miles to Lancer. Mike bought some groceries, and gassed up the truck. They loaded many cases of beer for the barn dance and were soon on their way home. When they arrived at the river they discovered that the ferry was on the far side of the river, but they could see no sign of the ferryman or anyone else.

As they waited, the minutes ticked slowly by. Mike suddenly realized that he had developed a compelling thirst, so he opened a case of beer. After he cranked one open for himself, he asked Walter if he would like one. Walter tentatively accepted the invitation even though he had never tasted this beverage. In any case it was a hot day and he was thirsty. His first taste was a big gulp. Tears immediately flooded his eyes as the bitter fluid swirled down his throat. Although it tasted awful, he was too polite to complain. The next swallow tasted much better, and by the fourth gulp he began to enjoy the heady beverage.

Fifteen minutes later, with still no ferryman in sight, Mike opened a couple more beers. Walter really relished his second beer, and it disappeared in a few minutes, leaving a warm, happy feeling in its wake. By the time the ferryman finally appeared, Walter had demolished several more beers, and was feeling no pain.

As soon as the truck rolled onto the ferry, Walter felt sick. He rushed to the railing and generously contributed to the contents of the Saskatchewan River. On the way from the ferry to the Coomb's farm, he fell fast asleep. Mike helped to hitch the horses to the water wagon. Thank goodness they had filled the tank before the Lancer trip. With some difficulty Walter clambered to the wagon seat.

If the horses had looked in poor spirits upon arrival at the farm that morning, they now looked downright mournful. They instinctively sensed that the trip home would test their strength and endurance. Five hundred gallons of water had been added to the load. They struggled and strained in their harnesses, almost to the breaking point before the tanker wagon began to move.

As the rig slowly left Mike Coomb's yard, Walter totally relaxed and fell asleep. The four horses continued to plod along without guidance. Eventually, they reached home base and stopped in front of the concrete reservoir, with their driver still asleep. Walter woke up with a start to discover his father looking up quizzically at him. As Walter dismounted, he was aware that his dad sniffed a few times. Harry was sure that his son smelled of stale beer and an upset stomach. He immediately tried to put on a severe face as he told Walter to fetch the cows for milking, but Walter was sure that there was a twinkle of humor in his dad's eyes.

Walter saddled a horse and headed out to the pasture. Just past the gate a jackrabbit jumped out in front of the horse, which shied immediately. Walter was thrown alongside the road, fortunately landing in tall dense grass. He was sure that he heard his dad howl with laughter.

Walter did indeed learn a lesson that day. For several years thereafter, he refused to drink any kind of booze. It was seven years later that he drank his next beer, to celebrate joining the R.C.A.F.

Conditions on the farm continued to go downhill and by 1934, Harry completely ran out of money, endurance and hope. He sold the livestock and worn-out farm machinery at an auction sale for two hundred dollars. The family then packed essentials and moved to Saskatoon.

Harry found work on a variety of jobs during the first few years. With the outbreak of war he obtained stable employment, and never again gave a second thought to hardscrabble farming.

Walter served overseas as a pilot with the RCAF, and eventually returned to Canada in good health. The thought never crossed his mind to pursue a future in farming.

Part IV

BOOZE AND BOOTLEGGERS

During The Great Depression, moonshiners and bootleggers were regarded by the law as criminals, and they were searched out relentlessly by the police. When I was a teenager, I was under the impression that chasing down illegal alcohol offenders was the *main* preoccupation of the police. I guess, in those days, there was probably a shortage of more serious crimes out in the boondocks of Saskatchewan.

My dad was of the opinion that arresting booze law-breakers usually did not make too much economic sense. In many cases, when someone was found guilty of a booze-related offence, they were too poor to pay a fine. As a consequence, they would be sent to prison where all expenses were paid by the government. In many instances, the prisoners enjoyed much higher quality meals and had better sanitary facilities than were ever available at home.

I think my dad adopted this view shortly after my Uncle Ed went to jail (see "Uncle Ed's Cafe").

The making and selling of moonshine allowed many impoverished families to eke out a living and keep body and soul together. Alcohol sold in government liquor stores was high priced because it was heavily taxed. On the other hand, home brewed alcohol was much more economically priced. It allowed our family to prepare an effective and enjoyable cough medicine (see "Cherry Bounce").

Of course, there was a dark side concerning the use and abuse of illegal alcohol. I purposely avoided delving into these aspects. Instead, I tried my best to amuse the reader. After you've read the last story of this chapter, I'd much sooner hear a quiet chuckle than see you reach for a Kleenex.

Cherry Bounce

Have you ever enjoyed the delightful flavour of cherry bounce? Have you ever heard of this depression-era home remedy? I don't know whether this soul-satisfying brew was in general use in Saskatchewan when I was just a lad. Our family never tried to find out. We kept very secretive about it, because its preparation and consumption were illegal.

Let me tell you how our family converted harsh tasting, home-brewed moonshine into a health-restoring delectable medicine. Yes, this process was a family effort, with every family member involved.

My father completed the first step in the cherry bounce operation. Under the cover of darkness he silently sneaked out into the night. He walked quickly and quietly toward the edge of town where he had prearranged to meet a farmer. Just beyond the cemetery, he halted and waited in a copse of willow and chokecherry. When he heard a horse and buggy approach, he stepped out in the road and identified himself to the driver. The transaction took only a few seconds. My father paid the farmer one dollar in exchange for a gallon of moonshine. He then silently returned home at a good pace, the jug clutched securely under his arm.

The next step was a healthy outdoor activity, and it involved most of the family. My mother, my two older sisters and I traipsed out to the bushland pastures west of town. Each of us was equipped with a small tin pail. Mother also carried a wicker basket containing a delicious picnic lunch.

Our quest was the wild pin cherry. This tiny bright red fruit was high in flavour but very sour. The cherries did not occur in clusters. Instead, they were sparsely distributed among the branches, and it took ages to pick a cupful. After an hour or so my sisters and I became bored with picking. Mother had foreseen this reaction, so she gathered us around her and opened the picnic basket before we lost interest entirely.

After a delicious lunch we would resume picking pin cherries for nearly an hour before packing it in. The total yield for the outing was usually around two quarts of pin cherries.

The next step in the process was the infusion of the cherry colour and flavour into a gallon of water. To accomplish this, my mother dropped the cherries into a cheese cloth bag, secured it with a string and placed the bag in a gallon of hot water. Then she added several cupfuls of white sugar to overcome the acrid flavour of the cherries.

She then deposited a couple of pieces of firewood in the stove firebox to make sure that an even heat would be sustained. She believed that this berry mixture should be gently simmered, but never boiled. While she busied herself elsewhere in the kitchen, she would ask one of us to carefully watch the pot. Usually she made bread. The combination of fresh baked bread and simmering cherries filled the kitchen with a glorious aroma.

The first tasting session took place as soon as the "infusion" had cooled down. All of us children were allowed to taste a teaspoon full. It was sweet and bursting with flavour.

Mother would allow the cherry sauce to cool over night before adding the illegal alcohol. She mixed it well and then bottled it in quart bottles. Having completed the process she would allow us another taste, this time only a few drops in a teaspoon. It was certainly the most flavourful medicine that I ever tasted.

She then stored the bottles of cherry bounce on her preserve shelves in the basement. She now had a year's supply of medicine to be used to cure coughs, sniffles, bronchitis, 'flu, catarrh and every other malady affecting the lungs and airways.

The dosage of this cherry bounce medicine varied with age. It was not administered to children under six years of age. My dad said that it might stunt their growth. A teaspoon of cherry bounce was allowed once you started to go to school, but genuine symptoms had to be in evidence. Once you became a teenager you were allowed an adult dose of one brimming tablespoon.

Soon after my sixteenth birthday, I seemed to have developed a strong liking for cherry bounce. The following winter I developed sniffles or a raspy throat with much greater frequency than ever before. It was about that time that my mother moved her supply of cherry bounce to a secret hiding place.

The Miller Twins

My friend Craig Miller, born and raised in Saskatoon, tells this story about how he and his twin brother, Paul, got into serious trouble just because their father enjoyed a combination of poetry reading and top quality moonshine. Here is the story as told by Craig.

Although it happened seventy years ago (1933), I still think that it was mainly our father's fault. I honestly believe that it was a mistake on his part to leave my twin brother, Paul, and me to our own devices upon our first visit to Larry O'Hara's farm.

After all, although we were only six years old, our father knew that his twin sons had already established a reputation as accomplished mischief makers. He also knew that this applied at home, or at school or just about anywhere. We seemed to have overactive, impish imaginations as well as a tendency to face challenges without regard to the consequences.

The problem started when our father took us with him one afternoon to Larry O'Hara's farm, about twenty miles west of Saskatoon. Dad really didn't want to take us that day. He wanted to enjoy Mr. O'Hara's companionship without any intrusions from two six-year-old hellions. He was more or less forced to take us. Our mother was leaving the city to visit a sick out-of-town relative. Paul and I were much too young and rambunctious to be left at home unattended.

A visit to Mr. O'Hara's farm presented a strong attraction to our father. Some years before he had discovered that his friend was a gifted poet, and that he also had a talent for reading his poems to an audience. He could put great expression and feeling into his recitals. Although he had emigrated from Ireland more than 25 years previously, his voice still carried a rich old-country brogue which sounded magical to our father, whose parents had come from Ireland a long time ago.

There was a second and equally compelling reason why our father enjoyed visiting Mr. O'Hara. Not only did Dad find delight in his poetry reading, he also appreciated a drink or two of the Irishman's double-distilled moonshine.

This was not the normal raw-tasting homebrew offered by a bootlegger. Mr. O'Hara aged his product for several years in five gallon oak kegs, during which time it acquired both the color and flavor of a first class brandy.

Soon after our arrival at the farm, Dad and Mr. O'Hara became absorbed in conversation. They completely ignored us. Paul and I just stood there. We didn't know what we were supposed to do. My brother spoke up first.

"What should Craig and I do while you guys have a visit?"

Dad didn't seem to hear Paul. There was no reply.

Then I posed the question, but in a much louder voice. "Hey, Dad, what the heck are we supposed to do while you two are having fun?"

Although I now had his attention, it was Mr. O'Hara who replied. "You boys can go outside and explore the farm. There are a lot of interesting animals here. There are cows. Lots of cows, because this is a dairy farm. There are also pigs and sheep and horses and chickens and cats and dogs. Plus, a brand new litter of kittens. The big barn has a lot of hay in the loft. You can jump around all you like. There are trees to climb in the gully below the barn. Stay out of trouble and I'll give you boys a treat when you return to the house."

Our ears perked up as soon as we heard Mr. O'Hara say the word "explore". Paul and I glanced knowingly at each other and an air of excitement began to build up. When we heard the word "treat" that became "the icing on the cake". Our spirits became supercharged, and we were ready for adventure.

We quickly exited the house through the kitchen and stepped out on the porch. From there we enjoyed a panoramic view of barns, pens, sheds, machinery and a tall metal tower with a huge windmill at the top.

Where should we begin to explore?

Paul got in the first word. "Why don't we first check out the hay loft in the big barn?"

I agreed and off we ran at full speed across the yard. We entered the barn and climbed the ladder to the hay loft. The hay loft was huge, and it was at least half full of hay. As we stood silent for a second, we heard a muted sound coming from a cardboard box near the wall. We investigated, and sure enough, we discovered the kittens that Mr. O'Hara had mentioned. They were very tiny, and had not yet opened their eyes. We quietly petted them for a few minutes. This moment was probably our most subdued behavior during the entire afternoon.

Then we climbed up the huge pile of hay and discovered a couple of ropes dangling from a beam high above. Great potential for a Tarzan episode. We continued clambering up the hay, holding the ends of the ropes. When we got to the top we each grasped a rope firmly and then launched out into space yelling like Tarzan. After swinging to the far end of the loft we released the ropes and crashed into a pile of hay. This "jungle game" was very tiring, so after four or five swings we decided to resume our exploration.

We looked down the hill behind the barn and saw the gully Mr. O'Hara had mentioned. At the very bottom there was a copse of trees and all sorts of bushes.

I turned to my brother and suggested, "Paul, why don't we go down there and climb some trees.? Maybe we'll find a bird's nest or something."

Paul immediately began to run down the slope to the gully. I joined in the race and we were out of breath by the time we reached the trees. As soon as we caught our breath, we each shinnied up a tree as fast as we could. There were no birds' nests so we began climbing down. About half way down, my foot slipped, and I fell, scratching my arm on some bushes when I landed.

We then made a tour of farm animals. We first visited the pig pen and watched several huge fat pigs with little red-rimmed eyes greedily munching their midday chow. We then stopped by the sheep pen. There were several very young lambs frisking about energetically in sharp contrast to the parents who were quite content to be in the shade.

Our attention was then drawn to the windmill which stood beside a huge watering trough. This was brand new to us. We had heard that windmills were used to pump water for livestock.

At the moment, the windmill was idle. Paul suggested, "Why don't we start this thing and pump some water?"

I pointed to a wooden lever about three feet long, and replied, "Maybe if we pull this piece of wood, it will start things going."

I had made an accurate guess, but we both had to pull very hard to activate the vanes of the windmill. The rod controlling the pumping action began to move up and down rhythmically with much creaking and scraping as metal rubbed against metal. In less than a minute, water began to gush forth onto the watering trough. For us, it was pure magic. We watched in wonderment as the trough gradually began filling. I could imagine horses and cows gathered around slurping up water to their hearts' content.

However, in a few minutes our interest began to fade. We got itchy feet and decided to explore some more. After shutting off the windmill, we headed toward a strange looking building about a hundred feet beyond the house. It was a very long structure, but less than three feet tall.

I speculated, "Paul, what do you think that strange building is used for?"

"I have no idea. It's so low, it can't be used by most farm animals. Maybe it's a chicken coop."

As we got nearer we realized that this low structure had been built over a deep excavation. Most of the usable space was below ground level. There were no windows. Later on we were told that this was an ice house.

During the winter huge blocks of ice were cut from a frozen lake and stored in this building. The ice was stored in the excavation for maximum insulating effect after which several feet of straw were applied to the top surface of the ice to provide additional protection. Apparently, this ice was used during the summer by the dairy farm for cooling the milk so it would be ready for shipment to Saskatoon. A sloping wooden roof protected the contents from exposure to the sun and from the rain. The ice house was accessed by a door at each end.

We entered the ice house and immediately enjoyed the cool and darkened atmosphere. There was more than two feet of straw on top of the ice, so we rolled around and threw bunches of straw at each other. We soon tired of this activity. Then Paul suggested:

"Let's pile up the straw in the shape of a volcano."

I agreed, and we soon built five volcanoes, each close to three feet tall, down the centre of the ice house.

The volcanoes looked realistic to me. They were certainly the right shape. However, Paul's overactive imagination again expressed itself.

"Why don't we cause a volcanic eruption. I think I'll sneak into the house and find some matches."

I wasn't too sure that this was a very good idea; but, I thought, "What the heck.. Let's have some fun."

After all, we really hadn't had too much excitement so far this afternoon.

We first lit up the middle volcano. In seconds there was a beautiful eruption. Then all hell broke loose. The flames quickly spread to the other volcanoes. Paul escaped through the door at one end and I got out the other, with flames licking at our heels.

Our father and Mr. O'Hara heard our screams and came rushing from the house. The fire was already too far advanced. It could not have been stopped even if we had fire hoses. The ice house was completely destroyed. Mr. O'Hara was furious. He would not even glance in our direction.

Fortunately, the punishment for our misdeed was not physical. However, all of our normal privileges were immediately suspended. Among other penalties, we had to forego Saturday cartoons at the movies for a month. This was our worst punishment.

About six months later, circumstances at home forced our father to again take us along on his next visit to the O'Hara farm. This time he would take no chances with our behaviour. Upon our arrival at the farm, he gave us a tongue-lashing which included some serious threats. He intended to keep us under observation. He insisted that we sit quietly on hard-seated, straight-backed wooden chairs during the poetry recital.

We were able to comply with his demands for about ten minutes, at which time the fidgeting and giggling commenced. Whenever I looked my brother in the eye, or the other way around, as our eyes met, we would both giggle. At first very, very quietly, but at each successive time the giggling got a little louder. Then I discovered that my chair had a slight squeak, so I did my best to aggravate it and magnify the sound.

Our conduct began to exasperate our father. His face gradually became red, and he lost his patience and his control. He rushed toward us and tweaked our ears painfully. My ears stung for a long time afterwards. Then he made us sit quietly on the floor, each of us in opposite corners of the room, facing the wall.

Then he snarled at us, "You little rascals have absolutely no regard for others. I'll tell you this, and you'd better listen. If there is so much as a peep out of either of you, I'll twist your ears completely off and feed them to Mr. O'Hara's pigs."

His warning struck home. We still remembered seeing Mr. O'Hara's pigs chomping loudly on their food. We didn't want our ears included on their menu.

This time we behaved ourselves, and the visit ended successfully.

I believe that my experience on Mr. O'Hara's farm accounts for my aversion to poetry in later years.

Uncle Ed's Cafe

"I can vaguely recall my mom and dad talking in hushed tones about Uncle Ed being in serious trouble. Something about going to jail. It was many years ago, probably around 1935."

I was speaking to my recently-discovered cousin Roberta, Uncle Ed's and Aunt Rose's only daughter. Our paths had never crossed until 1995. She was still very young when I left Saskatchewan in 1943 to become a logger in B.C.

When I mentioned "jail", she solemnly nodded her head and commented, "It happened before I was born."

And then she told me the whole story.

The construction of a CPR branch line to Prince Albert in 1929, prompted the establishment of a brand new community called St. Benedict. It was in the middle of nowhere, surrounded by thousands of acres of very productive farm land. My father had high hopes of establishing a successful business there. He constructed a building which would accommodate a café on the main street, with large living quarters in the rear.

The timing of his business venture could not have been more disastrous. He opened the Basin Lake cafe in 1930, just when the Depression was tightening its grip. The business never became profitable. Hardly anyone could afford to even buy a ham sandwich and a piece of pie. The main income from the cafe was from the sale of candy, ice cream, pop and cigarettes. My parents began taking in boarders to prevent bankruptcy. To keep afloat my dad had to sell the car. He couldn't afford to run it anyway.

In the evenings my dad would play cards with the boarders and any visitors who dropped in. You could truly call it a very informal penny ante poker club.

One evening one of the card players asked dad if there was any rye whiskey on the premises. Of course there was none! Who could afford such a luxury? Then he suggested that Dad keep a bottle of rye on hand and sell a generous drink to the card players at a reasonable but profitable price.

Mom and dad discussed this suggestion at great length, and finally made a desperate decision to give it a try. Their venture into bootlegging became an immediate success. Although they still operated on a tight budget, this added income helped them get by. Mom thought that it was very ironic that while it was nearly impossible to sell one of her delicious roast chicken dinners complete with trimmings, pie and coffee for 25 cents, you could more easily sell a generous shot of rye for 50 cents.

Unfortunately, this business expansion would lead to trouble. One summer day a car with two plain clothes RCMP appeared in town. One of our boarders spotted them and rushed to the cafe to warn my folks, but he was too late. One of the cops caught my mother rushing out the back door with several bottles of rye gathered up in her apron. My father was arrested and found guilty of bootlegging. The fine was one hundred dollars or thirty days in jail. He couldn't pay the fine so he was jailed for a month at Prince Albert. My mother continued to sell booze while he was away, but she had learned to be secretive about it.

While in prison, my dad was impressed by the quality of the meals. Although they were not as tasty as my mother served, they included a wide variety of food, much more varied than could be afforded by most people in the grip of the Depression.

As Roberta told this story, some other memories of those days began to take shape in my mind. I remember Uncle Ed as a very kind and generous person. I remember a visit to Uncle Ed's before I was old enough to start school, probably around 1930. We did not have many visits to St. Benedict because my dad could not afford to operate the car once the Depression took control of our livelihood.

I was the only boy in the family, and my Uncle Ed had "taken a shine to me". I remember him lifting me up and seating me on the counter immediately above the ice cream containers. He then removed the lids from the ice cream buckets and asked me to choose any flavour. I was very shy and I hesitated. Good thing I did, because I ended up with a scoop of every flavour in a huge bowl, instead of one flavour in a cone. On our next visit I hesitated again, this time with intent, not shyness. Again I was given the same treatment.

I was thoroughly convinced that during a depression every boy should have an Uncle like my Uncle Ed.

Still Waters Run Deep

Twelve-year-old Lou was herding about twenty cattle on the railway right-of-way. He was stuck with this boring job because he was younger and smaller than his two older brother, aged fourteen and fifteen, who ran the farm.

Their father had suffered a severe head injury in a farm accident a few years before, and now lived in an institution. He would never be able to work again. Soon after their father was taken away, Lou discovered that he had gravitated to a low-level position: he was assigned to do chores that were unattractive to his older brothers. He seemed to have inherited the job of manuring the barn. Also, he was considered first in line in weeding and watering (carrying buckets of water) and for collecting potato bugs (which he incinerated with coal oil). It was also his job to fill the kitchen wood box with firewood and to fetch water from the well for household use. If he didn't do a satisfactory job, he faced punishment from a switch wielded by an older brother.

Abuse by his brothers filled his heart with resentment, and this feeling stayed with him for many years. It was only after he had been in the army several years that he was able, eventually, to overlook the past, and accept his brothers as friends.

It was late summer in 1933 that Lou herded the cattle to the railway. The past few months had been hot and dry with hardly a drop of rain. Their own pasture had already been overgrazed and the decision was made to turn the cattle on to the still un-grazed railway right-of-way. Lou was told to make sure that the cattle did not encroach on the adjacent grain fields, especially on a neighbour's field of oats that was an exceptionally good crop.

As the cattle grazed, Lou reclined on a grassy bank and contemplated his situation. There were a hundred things that he would rather do than this stupid job. There was very little for him to do. No companionship. Just dumb animals by a railway track. He was totally bored.

He gazed slowly over the countryside. Across the railway track the land gently sloped downward toward a little slough. There was a thicket of willow and aspen trees beyond the slough. Lou decided to investigate and check out if there were any Saskatoon berries around. He had eaten very little. He would certainly enjoy a handful of these delicious berries.

Here is Lou's story of the events which followed:

As I entered the thicket I immediately became aware of a well-worn path leading into the densest part of the bush. I began following the path until I suddenly realized that the path did not continue past a certain point. I was mystified. I got down on my hands and knees and carefully examined the ground. I saw the straight edge of belting fabric. This proved to be the hinge of a trap-door about two feet square. I then found a small loop of rope which I pulled. The trapdoor opened, revealing a flight of steps leading to an underground chamber.

Obviously, someone had carefully excavated a big hole and just as carefully had hauled away the dirt that had been exhumed . The chamber was about eight feet by eight feet in floor area, and around six feet deep. A dark-coloured stove pipe pierced the roof and was wired to a willow stem about the same colour and size as the pipe.

At first, I was confused by the equipment I saw. There was a small-air tight stove covered by a huge metal pot and attached copper tubing which entered a cylindrical metal vessel. Many bottles filled with liquid were lined up on shelves which covered an entire wall of the chamber. I touched the stove but it was cold. Obviously, it had not been in use that day.

Realization finally hit me. I had heard my two oldest brothers talk about moonshine and bootleggers, and it seemed to me that I had stumbled on an illegal still. Up to this point in my life I had never tasted alcohol in any form. I'll never know why I decided to lift a full quart off a shelf. At the same time, I became very concerned that the owner of this still might return at any time, so I quickly climbed out, carefully closed the trapdoor, and with a bottle of hooch under my arm, I headed back to the railway track.

I opened the bottle and took a tiny, tentative sip. I did not like the caustic taste nor the dreadful smell. But for some strange, compelling reason I tried another sip. A warm glow began to spread from my stomach in all directions. I could understand why this liquid was called fire-water. It became less and less distasteful with each successive sip.

I eventually gulped a good-sized swig. That was the last thing I remembered. I passed out with my head resting blissfully on the railroad track.

Suddenly, I was roughly awakened by someone slapping my face. My two brothers had arrived. From their tirade I gathered that a neighbour had phoned to tell them that our cattle had invaded his oat field.

I had consumed about one quarter of the bottle, so my oldest brother brought it home, where he tasted the contents, and commenced to conspire. In those days a gallon of hooch was worth one dollar, and those were the days when a dollar was worth a lot. He questioned me closely about the still equipment and especially about liquid supplies. He then insisted that I show him the location. I had a feeling that he was going to make some money out of the situation. I had no choice but to lead the way to my discovery.

When I opened the trap door my brothers gasped at what they saw. There were three shelves, eight feet long with rows of gallon jugs full of moonshine. In no time at all they stripped the chamber of all its liquid contents. During the next month or two my brothers sold the moonshine to several Humboldt bootleggers. I know that they collected over twenty-five dollars, but did not even give me one red cent.

Eventually, we returned to the still to find that all the contents had been removed. My brothers became very sad.

As the years went by I became increasingly intolerant of alcohol until eventually in my thirties I became totally allergic to it. After consuming only one beer I would get a terrible headache. I really believe that this allergy problem stems from the day that a twelve-year-old farm boy went on a binge after discovering an underground moonshine still.

Smitty's Last Tea Party

"What a feeling of frustration! When I came to the shop this morning I discovered that I had run out of coffee and out of money at the same time."

This was Smitty's greeting to his first morning visitor at the blacksmith shop. The date was June 4th, 1931. The Great Depression had taken over control of Smitty's livelihood and of his life. His blacksmith business was now in shambles, almost completely wiped out.

Ever since he had acquired the business seven years previously, the shop had been a busy place. Not only was there plenty of blacksmith work, but the shop had become a place where visitors and customers often dropped in for a visit. The shop had become a sort of informal social centre, encouraged by Smitty who always kept a big pot of coffee ready.

Running out of coffee was a serious matter. Fortunately, Smitty's first visitor came to his rescue and purchased some coffee at a nearby store. After delivering the coffee to Smitty, he offered some advice. "I think that you'll have to economize if you want to keep our 'social club' alive. On the farm my wife has come up with a coffee substitute that costs us next to nothing. I'll bring some to the shop and let you try it out on your friends. It could save you a few bucks."

A few days later, his friend brought a big jar containing the coffee substitute. Smitty thought that the contents looked like normal coffee. His friend explained. "This 'ersatz' coffee is made from barley. First, my wife roasts the barley in the oven until it turns dark brown. After it cools off, she puts it through a coffee grinder. Very simple and very cheap."

The next day, Smitty prepared a one-gallon pot of this barley coffee. When it had brewed sufficiently he took a sip. He didn't like it. The taste was nowhere near the flavour of coffee.

His visitors didn't think much of it either. Fortunately, a "birthday buddy" saved the day. To celebrate his birthday he had brought a bottle of rye whiskey to the shop. He proceeded to spike each person's cup of barley coffee with a generous shot of Seagram's best. This enrichment greatly improved the drink, and promoted a lot of discussion. Before leaving the blacksmith shop that day, the "birthday boy" took Smitty aside and suggested, "I feel that you should think about keeping a bottle or two of rye whiskey handy in the shop. You could sell a good shot of whiskey for twenty-five cents, and we'd all be happy."

This proposition came as a shock to Smitty. He had never thought of undertaking an illegal venture. Perhaps it offered an opportunity for him to get back on his feet.

That evening, he visited Tina, his fiancée. In 1929 they had started to make plans for marriage, but the Depression had interfered. Smitty told her about the events of the day. She also recognized the business opportunity. If it proved successful, maybe they could resume their wedding plans. She began making plans to convert a blacksmith into a bootlegger.

Tina insisted that this illegal business should be conducted in a clean and cheerful environment; definitely not on a coffee stool around the forge. She accompanied Smitty to the blacksmith shop and selected a room which had been used to store all sorts of supplies. The room was dank and dirty. All surfaces were grimy and grubby. The place stank of spilled petroleum products.

Although Smitty could see nothing positive about this room, Tina immediately saw its potential. The room was certainly large enough. It would have to be thoroughly cleaned and decorated. For privacy, the window would be boarded up, and replaced by an overhead sky light.

It took Tina and Smitty and a few friends about a week to convert the storage room into an attractive "grog shop" where "clients" could relax in a friendly atmosphere.

Smitty's friends immediately took a shine to this remodeled social club. In the first week of business, Smitty netted over twenty bucks.

A few weeks later, the business took on a new twist. A farmer appeared at the blacksmith shop with a wagon load of equipment that required repairing. In confidence he took Smitty aside and made a proposition.

"As you can see, the repairs I need will require a lot of your time. I am broke, so I cannot pay you. Would you be interested in bartering for your work?"

Smitty replied, "I'm not sure what you mean."

"My wife and I do a lot of bartering. We deliver butter and eggs at the grocery store in exchange for sugar and flour and other essentials. Last year, I paid our doctor bill by providing him with several loads of firewood.

"I would like to make a similar deal with you. I distill illegal alcohol out in the bush. It's good tasting moonshine and it's safe to drink. Someone told me that you recently started a little bootlegging business. So I thought that you might be interested in bartering some blacksmith work for my high quality moonshine. If you mix it in the right proportions with rye whisky, no one will be the wiser."

Smitty thought over the proposition for a minute or two. He mused to himself, " If I could successfully dilute the rye whiskey with moonshine, I could make a pretty good profit."

He replied to the farmer, "The deal sounds okay to me. This repair job is probably worth about five gallons of booze."

The farmer walked to his wagon, dug into a pile of straw and pulled out five one-gallon jugs of colourless liquid. He had made the same estimate as Smitty.

None of Smitty's customers seemed to notice that the whiskey had been adulterated. The addition of the much cheaper moonshine immediately increased his profitability.

However, a dark cloud loomed on the horizon. Someone eventually squealed to the police about Smitty's illegal operation. Some of his friends suspected the hotel man, whose beer parlor business had been suffering ever since Smitty began bootlegging.

One day in mid-afternoon, two RCMP constables raided the blacksmith shop, after carefully noting that eight people had entered the premises two hours previously, and no one had left.

The policemen sneaked quietly into the blacksmith shop, and heard the sounds of conversation and laughter from behind a closed door. They suddenly burst into the cheerful little "grog shop" and grabbed a half bottle of booze from a table. Satisfied with this evidence, they arrested Smitty and charged him with bootlegging.

Most of the town folks figured Smitty would be found guilty and fined about fifty dollars, since it was his first offence. Plans were made to take up a collection and help him out. But a guilty verdict was not to be. The evidence had been stored in an unlocked cupboard in the RCMP office located in a government building which also contained two jail cells and offices for the secretary-treasurer of the municipality.

It so happened that a close friend of Smitty's did the janitorial work in this building. During the two week period between Smitty's arrest and his day in court, someone had tampered with the evidence.

Finally, Smitty's trial began. Behind the bench sat the Justice of the Peace, who just happened to be Tina's uncle.

The J.P. carefully listened to the information presented by the RCMP. He then asked the constable, "Have you established that this bottle contains alcohol?"

The police officer snorted indignantly. "What else could it be? There were seven or eight guys sitting around a table drinking this stuff. The room absolutely reeked of rye whiskey."

The J.P. sharply replied, "I've always understood that in police work nothing is assumed. Bring that bottle up here and I'll check it out."

He unscrewed the bottle cap and took a small whiff of the contents. He frowned slightly and his face took on a puzzled look. After pausing a few seconds he took a couple of very strong long-drawn sniffs, which could be heard as far back as the third row of seats, all occupied by Smitty's customers. As he screwed the cap back on the bottle, he gave the constable a piercing look and, in a loud voice, said, "Constable, do you call this rye whiskey?"

"Yessir" replied the constable with a puzzled look on his face.

The J.P. scowled and snorted, "It sure tastes like tea to me."

And indeed it was tea. Someone had poured out the rye whisky and substituted tea.

The constable took the bottle and sniffed several times. His neck turned red, and he gave Smitty a dirty look. The J.P. hit the table a smack with his gavel and declared, "Case dismissed for lack of evidence."

After the trial, Smitty met joyously with his friends. It was a celebration of straight coffee. Beneath the general feeling of happiness there was a note of sadness. They all realized that Smitty would have to stop his bootlegging operation. The police would certainly keep him under observation, and they would be very careful where they stored any evidence.

After his friends left, Smitty and Tina began thinking about their future. There was now an air of uncertainty which ruled out plans for almost anything. The prospects of marriage had suddenly taken a nose dive.

But good luck again appeared on the scene. A letter from a relative on Vancouver Island arrived with a job offer for Smitty. There was a job opening for an experienced blacksmith in a logging camp roundhouse where steam locomotives were repaired.

Smitty immediately sent a telegram of acceptance. A return wire the same day confirmed that he was hired.

Two days later, he and Tina packed their bags and headed for the coast.

Donald's Delicious Dandelion Drink

Among Mom's long list of chores which kept her busy from dawn to dusk, one stood out in a special category. This concerned the annual production of ten gallons of a very palatable dandelion wine. Each year a new batch would be produced, until eventually her children became teenagers and she ceased production.

This story concerns the production of a particular batch of dandelion wine during the early '30's. I think probably 1933. In the spring the pastures, cemeteries, school yards, ball fields and most road right-of-ways in Cudworth were ablaze with billions of dandelion flowers. It took at least a bushel of dandelion flowers (with no green sepals or stems allowed) to make ten gallons of wine.

Mom was pretty shrewd and she knew how to get the cooperation of her brood when confronted with chores aimed at providing for the common good. So instead of loading us up with pails and marching us out to the fields to laboriously pick pails and pails of flowers, she organized a picnic. She baked a fresh batch of cinnamon rolls, added a couple of bottles of homemade lemonade and announced that we were going on a dandelion picnic. We never walked more than a couple of blocks from our home to enjoy this excursion; however, the event took on a festive character.

The pails became filled with blossoms, our tummies with goodies, and everyone was happy.

On this particular dandelion-picking trek, our pre-school cousin Donald accompanied us. He had not yet achieved much status as a dandelion picker - but he sure liked cinnamon rolls and lemonade. Mom (Donald's Aunt Rose) was so pleased with his attitude and conduct that she told him he could come over and have a tiny taste of the dandelion wine when she bottled it.

Several months later the wine had achieved the bottling stage. True to her word, she invited Donald to the event. She even made sure that some cinnamon rolls were on hand.

Before commencing the bottling operation, Aunt Rose poured a teaspoon of the wine into a tiny glass and gave it to her favourite nephew. At first, Donald was very uncertain as to whether he would like it. He coaxed a few drops onto the tip of his tongue to test the taste. What a surprise! It tasted better that raspberry Jell-O which was his all-time favourite. He eagerly gulped down the contents of the glass.

A few minutes later there was a knock at the door, and Aunt Rose left her bottling job to talk to the visitor. By this time Donald had developed a liking for this delightful dandelion juice. The lure of the golden liquid overcame his shyness. With one watchful eye on Aunt Rose, who was completely pre-occupied in conversation with her visitor, and the other eye focused on the wine crock, he dipped his glass into the intoxicating brew. However, instead of taking just a teaspoon, he filled his glass (maybe two ounces) and gulped it down. His whole body began to tingle. He felt great!

Aunt Rose soon returned to the wine crock and resumed her bottling job. Wouldn't you know it! Another neighbour dropped by, and Aunt Rose again left the crock unattended to greet her at the kitchen door. As soon as her back was turned, Donald again filled his little glass and quaffed the elixir in two gulps. Aunt Rose was still engaged in neighbourly gossip, so while still in a thirst-quenching mood, Donald helped himself to yet another glass. When Aunt Rose returned to resume bottling, Donald began to feel a bit woozy.

It didn't take long for more symptoms to appear, but Aunt Rose took little notice. She was busy corking the bottles and cleaning up after bottling the wine. She did not notice that Donald was sitting absolutely motionless, his eyes unblinking as he stared into the distance. His face had lost colour and his freckles now stood out in bold contrast to the whiteness of his face.

After storing the wine in the cellar and cleaning her bottling utensils, Aunt Rose began preparing dinner. In those days, our biggest meal was eaten at noon. She took Donald by the hand and headed for the potato patch to sample the new crop. By this time, Donald was feeling somewhat light-headed. His legs didn't seem to want to go exactly where he intended. When he inadvertently stepped on a couple of lettuce plants, Aunt Rose glanced at him sharply, and with a hint of suspicion in her eyes, she tightened her grip on Donald's arm and guided him on a straighter path. Up to this point in time, she had not realized that Donald was under the influence of her dandelion wine. After all, she had given him only a single teaspoon.

She turned over a forkful of soil exposing over a dozen small potatoes. Donald, squatting on his haunches, stretched out his right arm and leaned forward to pick up the nearest potato. His centre of gravity shifted too far forward. He completely lost his balance and bashed his face in the dirt.

For a short time, Donald lay with his face in the dug-up potatoes. Then a sweet and gentle smile creased the corners of his mouth, and he started to giggle quietly. Aunt Rose suddenly twigged to the fact that her favourite nephew was completely under the influence of her highly treasured dandelion wine. In real terms, a very small glass had become a tumbler. She helped him to his feet, brushed off his clothes, and quickly returned to the kitchen with Donald in tow.

When we got home from school for dinner, we took turns walking Donald around the house, hopefully to sober him up.

To this day we don't know whether his mom, my Aunt Clara, ever found out about Donald's dandelion wine experience. However, as the years passed, Donald would occasionally drop by and ask about his Aunt Rose's dandelion juice.

Part V

KEEPING THE PEACE

I must admit that the collection of stories in this chapter is rather a mixed lot. This chapter merely served as a convenient place to include stories which just didn't seem to fit any where else in this collection. Still, they meant too much to me to allow their omission.

For instance, the story "Crime and Punishment". It has little in common with the other tales in this section. In fact, the story does not contain a real crime. However, in those long ago days when I experienced the consequences of petty or minor infractions at the altar, the disciplinary punishment imposed made me feel like a real criminal.

I'd like to make comment on "Two Years Less a Day". This story is a curious mixture of tragedy and gallows humor, but with a happy ending. Perhaps it is a first class example of the old saying that truth can indeed be stranger than fiction.

Tracks in the Snow

My father and his brother owned a general store in a small Saskatchewan town. Our family lived only four blocks from the store, and my father always walked to and from work.

Around noon, one day, as he neared home looking forward to his dinner, he suddenly became aware of a commotion down the street and turned toward the noise.

He saw two men arguing heatedly; one was riding a horse and the other was on foot. Suddenly, the horseman began violently swinging a club, repeatedly striking the other man on the head. This one-sided altercation lasted less than a minute. The horseman galloped away leaving the other man lying on the ground, bleeding and unconscious.

My father, not quite believing what he had just seen, quickly ran for help to the doctor's office nearby. Thankfully, the doctor was there, and the two of them raced back to the man lying in the street. However, nothing could be done to save the man and he died before they could get him to the hospital.

Once my father had a chance to think about it, he suddenly realized that he recognized both the victim and his murderer. He had seen them many times when they collected their mail at the post office in the general store.

As he was the only witness to the crime, it was his testimony in court that led to a conviction.

A few months later, the store was broken into through the back door and considerable merchandise was stolen. My dad and his brother were shocked. The store had been in operation for over a decade without ever experiencing a break-in.

Three months later, the back door was again forced, and more merchandise was taken. The police, after some consideration, began to suspect that perhaps relatives of the convicted murderer were the culprits: perhaps to get even with my dad for testifying at the trial. The RCMP prepared a list of these relatives.

The first winter snow fell one night toward the end of October. It was only a light dusting, less than a half an inch deep.

The next morning, when my father opened the store for business, he saw various items of merchandise scattered on the floor. The rear door was hanging on one of its hinges. There had been another break-in.

Dad walked to the open back door and looked outside. There in the snow, he saw the tracks of two men and a motor vehicle. He stared at those tracks for a few minutes, and then got an idea. He immediately phoned the RCMP office.

"This is Joe Schmidt. Our store was broken into again last night. But this time, the thieves have outsmarted themselves. They left their tracks in the snow. Perhaps if we immediately visited the people on your suspect list, we just might discover some other tracks that match these."

The constable arrived promptly, and they set out to investigate. The country road led them through harvested fields, displaying yellowish-grey stubble protruding through a very thin cover of snow. The sun was now well above the horizon. A clear sky promised that the weather would warm up today. Dad noticed that the snow on the road had already started to melt wherever it had been disturbed by traffic. They would have to hurry.

They found nothing of a suspicious nature at the first farm on the list. Nor did the second farm provide a clue. However, as they drove into the next farmyard on the list, my father noticed a dog sitting alertly in front of a straw stack a short distance from the farm buildings. He turned toward the police officer.

"Corporal, do you think perhaps that dog is on guard duty over there by the straw stack?"

The Corporal raised an eyebrow and headed toward the straw stack. On their way, they noticed a lot of foot prints in the snow leading back and forth to the stack. Then they saw that a small part of the straw stack had been recently disturbed in the area right behind the dog. The disturbed area was no longer covered by snow.

The officer picked up a stout pole from the ground and began to probe the straw stack. Sure enough, in a few minutes several boxes of merchandise were exposed and my dad was able to identify the contents as belonging to the store..

An arrest was made and justice took its inevitable course.

It was ironic that the thieves were caught because of the first autumn snow fall, and some clever police work. Especially, since later that day all the snow disappeared, along with any trail leading to the evidence.

The store never again experienced a break-in.

Crime and Punishment

In my home town (Cudworth, Saskatchewan) the sons of many Catholic parents were destined to become acolytes, or as we were more commonly known: altar boys. Being an altar boy added a different dimension to pre-teen and teenage years. It was meant to inject some degree of discipline and respect into a young lad's character.

Each Sunday, each altar boy would attend one of two masses: an ordinary short service at 8 a.m. or, a high mass at 10 a.m.. The high mass was a much longer service, accompanied by the choir, plus a long sermon which made sure that the priest's flock was headed in the right direction.

Since the high mass was at 10 a.m., it allowed both parishioners and altar boys the luxury of sleeping in. For altar boys, the duration of the service posed a degree of discomfort. An altar boy spent a substantial part of the service on his knees, with nothing to lean on. Back muscles became sore as well as leg muscles and tendons associated with kneeling.

Sometimes the priest's sermon would go on at great length. It seemed like for hours. While it may have been considered tolerable for a parishioner in a rear pew to doze momentarily or even snooze for a minute or two, an altar boy was expected to stay bright and alert at all times.

When I was an altar boy, we were subject to rigid rules of conduct. Some of these rules were even applied outside of church. In that category, smoking and the use of bad language were among the major offences.

Of course, we all know that rules and regulations are only effective if enforced. One of the prominent Catholic citizens, Mr. C___, was the "enforcer" during my time as altar boy. He seemed to regard young teenagers as little monsters, always expecting the worst of them. Occasionally he got what he expected. I don't think he had children. He sure didn't have warm feelings for kids.

Mr. C___ was responsible for observing the conduct of the altar boys during church services. Giggling, whispering, fidgeting, and nose-picking were absolutely taboo. Outside of the church he also kept one ear cocked in case he might hear something negative concerning one of his charges. Mr. C___ took his duties very seriously.

Enforcement of these rules could result in expulsion from the altar boys' fraternity when there were extreme behaviour problems. A lesser infraction usually resulted in being sentenced to serving mass on weekdays. This was considered a form of punishment because you had to get out of bed two hours earlier than normal in order to attend weekday mass at 7:00 a.m..

One Sunday morning during high mass, I also violated a fairly serious rule of conduct. I was guilty of chewing gum. Just before the service began, one of the other altar boys shared his stick of gum with me. During mass I refrained from chewing to avoid detection whenever I faced the congregation. I slipped up only once, and wouldn't you know it, Mr. C___ occupied a seat in the front row, and he witnessed my misbehaviour. I knew it immediately, because our eyes met, and his eyes glinted in a very accusatory way.

That afternoon Mr. C___ visited our home and gleefully told my parents about my gum-chewing crime. Then he turned to me and said, "Ralph, for your disgraceful conduct you will serve mass on weekdays for two weeks."

I wouldn't have minded so much if it had been in summer. During that season I didn't mind getting up at the ungodly hour of 5:45 a.m.. The morning breezes were usually balmy, and the birds were singing. The summer dawn often brought a colourful sunrise if there was a partial screening of clouds to the east. But, unfortunately, I had chewed gum in early January. I would have to get out of bed in total darkness, in almost Arctic conditions every single weekday for two whole weeks. It was indeed a severe form of punishment to have to rise from bed in an ice cold bedroom, hastily gather up an armload of clothing, and scamper into the front room to dress by a coal-fired heater. On really frigid mornings my teeth would not stop chattering until after I had slipped into my long fleece-lined underwear and heavy home-knit woollen socks.

After eating a bowl of piping hot porridge, I would bundle up and step outside into total darkness and often bitter cold. Some mornings I stumbled to church through the snow in almost- blizzard conditions. If there was a strong north wind, I would walk to church backwards.

In sharp contrast to Mr. C___'s hard boiled personality, our priest, Father Casimer, was a very easy-going, gentle person who always had a kind word for everyone, but especially for his troupe of altar boys. We all admired him and showed him great respect.

Each Sunday, a few minutes before high mass, two altar boys were selected by Father Casimer to ring the church bells. There would be an exuberant race from the sacristy to the bell tower at the church entrance. The winner of the race grabbed the rope which controlled the big bell. Vigorous pulling on this rope gave the big bell some momentum. By hanging onto the rope you got a "yo-yo" ride. It was one of the best bits of fun to be had on a Sunday morning for an altar boy.

Another bright moment in the life of an altar boy was the opportunity to occasionally earn a little money. At both weddings and funerals we were paid a small fee, usually a quarter each. When the wedding ceremony was completed, two altar boys would scamper to the church entrance and hold the priest's rope sash across the doorway. This prevented the exit of the wedding party until the groom obliged us with a small donation.

We also received a small stipend for serving mass at funerals. A summer funeral presented few adversities. Funerals were usually conducted in the morning before the day became too warm. The leisurely procession from the church to the cemetery (nearly a half mile away) was accompanied by the songs of the birds and the smell of wild flowers. The final graveside ceremony proceeded at a relaxed pace. The funeral procession left the cemetery with a satisfied feeling. The ceremony had been conducted with benevolence and great consideration for the bereaved.

In contrast, a winter funeral could be a major challenge. The procession from church to cemetery during near-blizzard conditions reminded me of pictures I had seen of Napoleon's army retreating from Russia.

The priest and five or six altar boys led the procession, their black gowns fluttering like the tattered flags of a vanquished army. Next in the procession plodded a team of sad-looking horses pulling a sled carrying the coffin. There was no sign of gayety. The horses did not even wear harness bells. This "hearse" was followed by relatives and friends of the deceased, all bundled up in fur caps with ear flaps or huge toques, heavy woollen scarves, long thick winter coats, mittens and overshoes. From time to time they flapped their arms to stay warm. Sometimes in the frigid cold, certain phrases were uttered , and not just by the alter boys, which were not in keeping with church services of any kind.

Outside of the bitter cold, the most outstanding characteristic of a winter funeral was its brevity. You simply could not tarry at the graveside in frigid weather. All of the required ceremonies at the grave were observed but at a very lively pace. Once the very last "Amen" was uttered the entire crowd departed as quickly as possible. Older parishioners maintained a brisk but moderate pace. The younger generation, with the altar boys in the lead, scampered helter-skelter through the snow to return to the warmth of the church to treat their frost-bitten extremities.

On looking back to my teen-age years, I still think quite positively of my altar boy experiences. Certainly that segment of my life served as a counter balance to teen-age experiences of a logger in B.C., and an airman in the RCAF.

Two Years Less a Day

Since socially unacceptable behaviour is involved, I cannot use real names in this anecdote.

During the 1930's, Joe M. had become a solid pillar of the community, an average size town in eastern Saskatchewan. The town was distinguished by the number of churches (five); the number of grain elevators (seven); the size of the curling rink (four sheets) and the size of the livery stable which could accommodate a hundred horses.

Joe was the secretary-treasurer of the municipality with an office in a small brick building which had housed a flourishing bank business before the Depression. Joe's fellow citizens regarded him as a paragon of honour and trust. He was always willing to help others whenever he could. He actively participated in community affairs and projects. If you had a problem, discuss it with Joe, and he'd probably help you solve it. You just could not say enough praiseworthy things about him.

No one in the town knew that Joe harboured a very disgraceful secret. In fact, he had two secrets which were completely at variance with the townspeople's perception of him. His primary hidden vice was booze, and it had led directly to the second, which was corruption.

It had been only during the last couple of years since his wife had died that he had been drinking heavily, and always alone. Eventually the habit had become an addiction.

In order to maintain a reputation of respect, integrity and temperance, Joe went out of his way to keep his drinking habit well hidden from public view. He purchased liquor at another town, several cases at a time. Consequently, his fellow citizens never saw him in the local liquor store. As his consumption of alcohol increased, so did its cost. At one point in time he played with the idea of switching from expensive government liquor to very cheap moonshine mostly distilled by "hill-billy" farmers who laboured hard to make an "honest" living. He had tested this home brew a few times in the past, and he disliked the taste, even when it was doctored up with 7-Up or some other mixer. He was also fearful of the quality. His good friend, the RCMP corporal had cited figures of the numbers of people who had been poisoned by moonshine with a high content of fusel oil.

Joe also disposed of his empty liquor bottles in a secretive manner. When he first moved his office into the abandoned bank building a few years previously, he was astounded at the size of the bank vault. In fact, a friend had suggested that it was big enough to house a flock of chickens with plenty of room left over for a cow or horse. He used this space to store "dead soldiers" as Joe called the cases of empty liquor bottles . Although his booze consumption was high it would take years to fill the available space.

Some background information is needed to set the stage for subsequent events. During the Depression the federal government provided a small old-age pension to eligible seniors. However, the law made it clear that you could not collect this pension if you had a bank account. Quite a number of old-timers in the area had been financially successful during the 1920's, and they had significant balances in their savings accounts. Joe made it known that he would protect their savings by storing their money in the disused bank vault which was big enough for a flock of chickens. This protection was attractive, and in a short time Joe was safekeeping a considerable amount of cash.

One morning after waking up with a slight hangover, Joe realized that he had a serious financial problem. He was broke. His booze supply had been totally depleted. Payday was still a couple of weeks away. And worst of all, the OAP funds that he had held in trust had been entirely spent to purchase booze. He was in desperate need of a considerable amount of cash to replace the OAP funds and to lay in a supply of booze.

Gradually a plan began to form in his mind.

The only significant amounts of cash were on deposit in the banks. He dealt with a bank in a town about fifteen miles away. Why not rob this bank and replenish his finances? He knew that there were always thousands of dollars in their vault, and hardly any security. The more he thought about this venture the better he liked it. Although it was mid-morning, he locked his office and walked home. He sorted through the pots and pans and selected a big aluminum pot which easily fit over his head. After twenty minutes in his workshop, he emerged with two eye-holes cut in the pot. He tried it on. He had unrestricted vision with the pot resting gently on his shoulders. He was confident that no one would recognize him.

My curling friend Ken told me this story. At the time he was completing grade eleven and working part time at a lumber yard in this town. On the day of the bank robbery, Ken was tidying up the office, while listening to music from a small radio. Suddenly an urgent announcement interrupted the music. A lone criminal had robbed the bank in a neighbouring town and made off with several thousand dollars. The police did not have a good description of the culprit. But they said that he had a distinctive English accent, and they announced the licence number of his car. When Ken heard this report he wrote down the licence number.

A few minutes later Joe's son dropped in. Ken asked, "Did you hear about the bank robbery?'

"What bank robbery?" was the reply.

Ken reiterated the details he had heard on the radio, and then told him that he had written down the car licence number. Joe's son trembled when he saw the licence number and he said, "My God, that's the licence of my dad's car."

Instead of returning home after the holdup, Joe took a well-planned detour. After driving a few miles out of town, he turned onto a seldom-used road that wound its way through hilly land that was not under cultivation. When he saw no evidence of any traffic, he left the road and followed an old wagon trail that wandered through a grove of white poplar and willow. He stopped the car when he was beyond the view of anyone who might be traveling on the road.

He removed a shovel from the car and dug a hole where he buried the aluminum pot which he had used for a disguise. He then carefully packaged the stolen money in a cardboard box which he secured with strong cord. When he passed through the next town, he stopped at the Post Office and mailed the parcel to his secretary-treasurer office. As he drove home he felt rather smug because he no longer possessed evidence of his crime.

The news of the robbery spread like wildfire. There was no doubt about the identity of the perpetrator. The bank teller had recognized Joe's pronounced Yorkshire accent, and in fact, she initially thought the whole episode was a joke. In checking out the car licence the police constable immediately identified the car owner. However, he had a problem. He was a close friend of Joe's. They played bridge once a week. They were elders of the same church. They often worked together raising money for charity. The constable simply could not bring Joe into the clutches of the law. In the end he asked Joe's son to bring his dad to the police station.

It took a couple of weeks before the case came to court. Meanwhile, several pensioners needed money. Joe's son unlocked his dad's office. He knew that his father kept some money in the dis-used bank vault. To his surprise he discovered that the vault was piled high with boxes full of empty liquor bottles. It was the first inkling that his father was an alcoholic. Then he discovered that the pension accounts were empty - not a penny remained!

Joe was found guilty - in fact he pleaded guilty. A sympathetic judge sentenced him to two years less a day so that he did not have to do time in a federal penitentiary. After settling down in prison, Joe decided to turn a new leaf. Of course he had to give up booze. But he also decided to do something positive. He planned to write a book. A year and a half later it was published. It was a humorous story entitled "How Not to Rob a Bank"

Meanwhile, Ken joined the RCAF and lost track of Joe, although he did hear that the book had become a real money maker, and allowed Joe to pay back the money he had so conveniently "borrowed" from the pensioners.

Moonshine Madness

Human beings consume alcohol for various reasons. Some people even drink it because they are thirsty. However, when too much is consumed at one sitting the results are often unpredictable. Their drunken antics make no sense whatever.

On the prairies during the Depression the production and sale of illegal moonshine was often a venture of last resort. Some farmers turned to this activity to generate some cash. You could produce eggs and butter and barter them to a general store for sugar and flour and other essentials. However, you needed cold hard cash to patronize the Eaton's catalogue or your local hardware store.

For sure, moonshine, also known as homebrew or white lightning, was rated as one of the most popular alcoholic beverages on the prairies at that time. It gained this popularity because in addition to its high alcohol content it was abundantly available and very cheap. Around my home town (Cudworth, Saskatchewan) there were many bootleggers and you could buy a quart of this heady illegal elixir for thirty cents if you bought it directly from the producer.

Judging by the results, the prairie homebrew was very potent, containing more "devilish spirits" than much more expensive hard liquor purchased at the government liquor store. Whether this could be attributed more to the quality of the water (usually as hard as a rock) or the makeup of the mash, or the TLC of dedicated prairie farmers, we'll probably never discover. However, we do know that overindulgence often produced very foolish and sometimes foolhardy behaviour.

Here is a story told to me by a friend who spent his childhood and youth in a small town in southeast Saskatchewan. (There are too many living relatives to use real names.)

The story revolves around Roddy, an Icelander who had a passion for prairie moonshine. He was a capable and diligent carpenter who built fine homes and many serviceable farm buildings. On occasion he would even build furniture. After working steadily for several weeks, he would feel the need to "kick off the traces" and go on a "bender".

He would drink moonshine straight, or mixed with water or fruit juice or 7Up or in any other way. He also liked to let the whole town know just how much he enjoyed this illegal potion.

Once he had achieved an advanced state of drunkenness he would round-up his twelve gauge shotgun from a closet in his bedroom, load one shell of bird shot in the chamber and six in the magazine. With his weapon held firmly under his right arm he would lurch out the doorway onto the street and stagger down the middle of the road, heading for the downtown area.

After he had tottered and wobbled about a block he would stop, lift his gun to his shoulder, cock it, aim it at the sky above , and pull the trigger. Sometimes if he had grossly exceeded his booze capacity, the recoil was sufficient to knock him on his hind quarters. He would rise unsteadily to his feet, slap at his dusty pants a few times, pick up his artillery and commence to swerve and shuffle for another fifty paces or so. Then he would stop again, point the gun skyward and fire another shot. He continued along his faltering and unsteady path, stopping every few minutes to fire his weapon, fall in a heap and rise again.

The local citizenry was very familiar with Roddy's antics on these occasions. After hearing the first shotgun blast, they would drop whatever they were doing and listen attentively, their mouths agape and their eyes staring widely and unblinking as they very carefully counted each shot.

After seven shots had reverberated between the town hall and the grain elevators, they knew the gun was empty, and four or five of them would rush onto the street, overcome Roddy physically and carry him to the local jail for an overnight stay.

The next day Roddy would awake with one heck of an Icelandic hangover, begging for a large mug of black coffee and a cold wet towel to wrap around his head.

Most of the time Roddy was a well-liked and respectable citizen. In fact, the Justice of the Peace was so sympathetic toward him that he would set a token fine of two dollars and fifty cents for disturbing the peace.

Each time that Roddy was put on charge for disturbing the peace, the J.P. would end up the proceedings by delivering a message to Roddy:

"Roddy, we all know that you go out on a toot every month or two. Each time you are fined for your bad behaviour. If you changed your habits slightly we would all be better off. Instead of paying a fine for misbehaving, you could spend the money saved on the purchase of legal government hard liquor instead. I am sure that you would live longer and suffer less if you avoided drinking rotgut homebrew.

"Instead of making a nuisance of yourself with that shotgun I suggest you give it to the mayor to auction off for charity. With no gun available you would pose no problem to the peace of this community and avoid jail, hangover and a fine."

This message seemed to pass over Roddy's head with little notice. Somehow the prairie moonshine had him in its grip.

However, Roddy always had the last word. "Your Honour, the trouble with this country is that we are all under the marketing control of Ontario. In actual fact you should be telling prairie people to change their habits. Instead of buying high-priced canned food and booze from back east, they should eat more bread and eggs and beef produced right here. Moreover, the hard liquor from Ontario cannot compare in price with our local product. As you can see I am doing my utmost to bring prosperity back, by drinking more than my share of prairie moonshine."

One Dime, Three Nickels, and Two Pennies

My friend, John Striha, who provided me with a hobo story, also gave me this bootlegger tale.

Mike and Maria plus their eighteen-year old son Tony had farmed near Moose Jaw since arriving in Canada from Rumania ten years previously. The first few years of the Depression had been difficult, but somehow they had managed. However, their luck had suddenly run out last year. Drought and dust storms were followed by crop failure. The farm had not even produced enough feed for their livestock. They now owned only one team of horses, which roamed at will for forage, and about a dozen chickens which did the same.

Maria Chenescu glanced soberly at her husband as he entered the kitchen.

"Mike, we're completely out of sugar. And I'm going to need yeast or there won't be any bread this week."

Mike acknowledged Maria with a nod of his head and sat down glumly at the kitchen table. Then he added another item to her shopping list.

"We are also out of kerosene for the lantern and the lamps."

All was silent for several minutes; then Mike sighed heavily and mumbled, "Maria, we're in real trouble. Last week the store keeper complained that our bill was getting too big. We haven't paid anything on it for over a year. He told me that he could not carry us much longer. Maybe we could find a little money in the house to buy a few groceries."

Maria replied in a quiet voice, "I don't think I can find very much, but I'll look anyway."

Maria left the kitchen and started searching for money in their bedroom. At the bottom of her purse she found a nickel and two pennies. Then she checked the pockets of her husband's clothes in the closet and found one dime in his Sunday suit. She returned to the kitchen and checked through the cupboard. Behind a stack of plates she discovered two nickels. She now had a total of twenty-seven cents.

She gave the coins to Mike. He glanced down at the coins in the palm of his hand. There they were: a dime, three nickels and two pennies. These six coins were the total purchasing power of his family.

He spoke to Maria in a strained voice. "If things don't get any better we just might have to abandon the farm. I've got to find a way to earn some money."

Then he thought of his cousin Peter who had gone broke two years ago farming north of Regina. Peter had managed to survive by distilling moonshine and peddling it to bootleggers in town. He wasn't rich, but he was slowly getting back on his feet.

Mike told Maria, "Maybe I should make homebrew. I'm sure Peter would help me get started."

Maria responded, "Bootlegging is illegal, and you know it. You've never done a crooked thing in your life. You want to go to jail?"

Mike felt too desperate to think about getting caught by the law. Morally, he felt on safe ground. He was sure that to most ordinary people in Saskatchewan bootlegging was a very low-cost convenience, especially on birthdays, dance nights and weddings. It was as much a part of prairie life as dust storms, grasshoppers and crop failure. On the other hand, he also knew that the government was very much against bootlegging. Booze purchased at a government liquor store produced a big tax dollar, but bootleggers contributed absolutely nothing to government coffers. It was for this reason the Mounties spent much of their time on the hunt for bootleggers.

Mike contacted his cousin Peter who offered encouragement and promised to help him get started. They established the brewing operation far out in the pasture, a half mile from the house. The equipment was well hidden among a cluster of willow trees in a small coulee.

Mike had no difficulty in selling his home brew. In fact, demand usually exceeded supply. Gradually, economic conditions improved in the Chenescu household.

One year in mid-September, he was approached by a local bootlegger who had just started to sell in quantity to a big distributor in Moose Jaw.

"Mike, I need more homebrew if I'm going to stay in business."

Mike had a disappointing answer, "I don't have any on hand and I can't process the mash until next spring. It's too cold outside for fermentation."

"I would pay you a better price, and pay cash for all you can make."

It was too big a temptation for Mike. He decided to ferment the mash in the kitchen, despite Maria's objections. Mike placed a barrel two-thirds full of mash right next to the kitchen stove, and fermentation proceeded at a rapid rate.

Maria nervously kept a wary eye out for any sight of traffic on the narrow road leading to their farmyard.

One day, when she was fetching a pail of water from the well, she saw a plume of dust rising in the distance. It was a car, and it was being driven as fast as the road would permit. She immediately abandoned the pail, ran to the house, and yelled, "Mike, I think the police are coming!"

Mike scrambled to his feet and rushed outside. One look at the fast approaching vehicle convinced him. He called to his son. "Tony, come quick! The police are coming. I need your help!"

Mike decided to get rid of the fermenting mash. The barrel was much too heavy to lift. Instead, he and Tony tilted the barrel and rocked it from side to side, gradually inching it toward the kitchen door. It was slow work.

They finally reached the doorway just as a Mountie bounded up the porch steps. When he saw Mike and Tony manipulating the barrel, he knew he had to stop them. He braced himself and a pushing struggle began.

However, the Mountie was no match for the combined strength of father and son. Slowly, but surely, the barrel was being tilted to the point of no return. With one final heave they tipped the barrel just as the Mountie's footing gave way. His left leg slipped and the lip of the barrel caught the Mountie just below the knee and tore the skin from his shin. To add insult to injury, about five gallons of warm, reeking mash sloshed down his injured leg, which was already burning with pain.

The contents of the barrel were being quickly absorbed by the parched ground alongside the porch. There was no longer one ounce of evidence for the Mountie to collect.

The Mountie struggled painfully to his feet spluttering several choice words in the process. He then made a quick search of the premises, found no trace of home brew, and limped out to his car.

The next day, the Mountie returned and, with a satisfied smirk on his face, he served a summons. Mike had been charged with assault and battery. No mention of any bootlegging infraction.

A month later, Mike appeared before a judge. The judge had been briefed on the case a few minutes previously. He was aware that the Mountie had been seeking evidence to catch a bootlegger, and that he had not been successful.

Mike stood before the judge wearing a patched and faded shirt with frayed collar and cuffs, and worn-out overalls displaying several patches. The judge could plainly see that here was just another poor farmer, and he felt some compassion toward him.

"So, Mr. Chenescu, what do you have to say to this charge? Are you innocent or guilty? Assaulting a police officer is a very serious matter. Did you attack this Mountie in the pursuit of his duty?"

Mike could speak English pretty well, but he chose to purposely reply in broken English. Maybe the judge would feel sorry for a poor immigrant farmer.

Mike rose from his seat and began talking. "Judge, we wary poor pipple. No money to buyink lottsa stuff. We growink our food. We makink our food, cookink, bakink. The day this crazy policeman attackink me, we gonna put sauerkraut in barrel. First, to clean barrel, my son Tony is halpink. We movink barrel to doorway to dumpink dorty cleanink water outside in sunflowers. Same time is comink crazy policeman and stoppink us. I no understand."

At this point, the judge interupted, "Just a minute, please. Exactly what do you mean by crazy policeman?"

Mike responded immediately with fire in his eye, and said, "He's actink like wild animal, yallink, pushink, jumpink all ower the place. " There was a brief pause and Mike continued, "Anyway, crazy policeman jumpink on porch too fast, is slippink on wet step, and cuttink leg on boot cleaner."

Again the judge interjected, "Would you please explain?"

Mike responded in his broken English. "You know. Boot cleaner is metal piece fastened to porch to cleanink cow shit from boots."

Mike paused for a few seconds and then continued on a sympathetic note, "Crazy policeman has bad cut. Maybe gonna be blood poison happen."

Again he paused and then added his final two cents worth. "I'm not puttink one finger on crazy policeman. Not once even touchink to him. You callink assault? I don't believink. Maybe crazy policeman should goink to jail for sayink bad words in front of my Maria."

Mike sat down and folded his arms. He was finished with his testimony.

The judge closed his eyes for a minute and leaned back in his chair. He really didn't believe the sauerkraut story. Somchow, it didn't ring true. On the other hand, the Mountie could have slipped and fallen on his own. There was no substantial evidence to the contrary. There were no other witnesses.

He also realized that the Mountie's pride had been injured more than his leg.

He rapped the bench solidly with his gavel, laid it quietly beside the inkwell, and in a stern voice uttered, " Case dismissed for lack of evidence."

Part VI

BLIZZARDS

I have not experienced a prairie blizzard for sixty years. However, clear memories still linger. If I choose a quiet corner, and close my eyes and concentrate, I can hear the wind shrieking at full strength and feel the bite of the cold. Despite a lapse of six decades, I can still visualize streamers of powdery snow being powered through the air with amazing velocity. I can also recall the alarming reality of a total white-out when all familiar land marks disappear from view.

"Saved by the Bells" is my favourite story in this chapter. I think it brings home the drama that accompanies desperation and rescue during a life-threatening winter storm.

I hope you enjoy reading these stories. I enjoyed bringing them to you.

My Lofty Library

As I grew up in small town Saskatchewan during the 1930's, I gradually became a fervent, addicted, all-consuming reader. This accomplishment was almost inevitable, considering the circumstances.

There were many contributing factors: long, cold, winter nights; no brotherly companionship (I had only sisters, a grand total of four!); an old-fashioned battery-powered radio seldom in use (occasionally, we could afford a battery charge); and eventual boredom with checkers, Parcheesi and card games.

A good book meant many things to me. It added a special zest to my life, like the icing on a cake. It could be both a friendly companion as well as a staunch friend. Often, it provided a flight of fancy which stimulated my innermost spirit. I could not imagine a life where reading was not a vital component.

After supper, my homework always came first. Fortunately, I was usually able to cope with this obligation in short order. After I closed my schoolbooks, I was ready to read.

Unfortunately, fresh reading material was not always available. Our town did not have a public library. Our school library consisted of one cupboard, mostly displaying bare shelves. I don't think this "library" contained more than twenty well-worn, dog-eared books.

One bright spot on my reading horizon was a library owned by the Junior C.W.L. (Catholic Woman's League). Members of the C.W.L. took turns housing and managing this library. For several years, it found a home in our house, where my two oldest sisters took on this responsibility. This library contained around fifty carefully selected books, approved by the church. I enjoyed reading every book in this library; some I read twice. My favourite author was James Oliver Curwood. His action-packed adventure stories always thrilled me.

Although our family was not well off, my father allowed himself the luxury of subscribing to the Winnipeg Free Press, and to a western magazine packed with cowboy stories. When a new issue arrived, I would read the entire magazine from cover to cover, long before my dad was half finished. The Winnipeg Free Press was a small-paged weekly newspaper. At times, I was so desperate for reading material that I would even read all of the want ads.

Yes, I was always on the lookout for more reading material. In 1942, when I turned seventeen, my efforts were unexpectedly rewarded. A supply of reading materials suddenly appeared as a result of my dad's decision to insulate the ceiling of our house.

This decision followed closely after an abnormally cold and prolonged blizzard.

It was after supper one evening that my dad asked my mom, "Rose, can you remember ever having such a cold spell as we just lived through?"

Mom though for a moment, "Not unless it was during my family's first winter in Saskatchewan over twenty years ago. Our home on the farm wasn't air tight. There were icy drafts in every room; even we girls wore fleece-lined long-johns."

Dad continued, "Anyway, the Monarch Lumber Yard agent told me today that he had received a box car load of white spruce chips from a planer mill in Prince Albert. Also, that these chips would make real effective insulating material."

And so it followed, that for several days after school I hauled wood chips home in big gunny sacks on my bob sled.

Climbing into the attic to distribute the chips was not an easy matter. The entrance to the attic was a square hole in the middle of the room. Since we had no step ladder, we moved the dining room table a couple of feet and then place a chair on the table.

I was the first to enter the attic. My dad held the chair securely while I clambered up.

Dad warned me: "Be careful where you step. If you put your feet between the ceiling joists, you'll come right through the ceiling. You better stand on the ship-lap walkway down the middle."

After entering the attic, I slowly beamed a flashlight around this tent-shaped room. It was a gloomy-looking place with dusty, long-trailing cobwebs draped from every single rafter. We were going to have to use a broom before we could tackle our job. When I aimed the flashlight near the chimney, I detected a pile of dust-laden cardboard boxes.

By this time, my dad had joined me and I asked, "What is stored in those boxes?"

My dad smiled and responded, "By golly, I had completely forgotten. Years ago, I used to save every magazine that I read. I remember packing them carefully into cardboard boxes, and storing them up here."

There were five boxes in all, and we carefully lowered them to the dining room.

Dad and I worked a couple of hours, spreading the wood chips evenly and thickly between the joists. The work went too slowly for me. I was eager to examine the contents of the boxes.

Finally, we finished the job and climbed down to the dining room. I was filthy. I had to change clothes and wash up before I could look at the boxes.

The magazines had been carefully packed in chronological order. They were clean and in almost "mint" condition. What a discovery! There was a complete set of Argosy magazines from 1919 to 1929 and a matching set of cowboy magazines.

I decided that this unexpected bonanza of reading material would have to last me until spring. I would resist the urge to indulge in a "reading binge" where I might consume all of these magazines before the frost had left the ground in spring.

First, I counted the magazines, and then I counted the days until spring. I prepared a reading schedule based on these figures. They were going to last me the rest of the winter!

And they did. In fact, I read the very last story of the last magazine during my last evening in Saskatchewan. The next day, I departed on the CNR mainline train from Saskatoon and headed west to become a logger on Vancouver Island.

Occasionally, I have thought about the enjoyment that these magazines provided so many winters ago. Did my father again place them in the attic after I left Saskatchewan? Perhaps there is still a library in the attic of the little house where I was raised; if so, these eighty-year-old magazines would surely be collectors items now.

Our family never did find out if the wood chip insulation was effective. The next winter, all of us were living in B.C. We never again experienced a Saskatchewan blizzard.

The Remittance Weatherman

John_______ died at Vegreville, Alberta in January, 1934. His obituary was very brief. There were only two statements concerning his past:

"This kind and gentle remittance man emigrated from England to a ranch in southern Alberta in 1898 at the age of twenty. He joined the cavalry in 1914 and served overseas."

John had been a very private person. He did mention that after the war he had returned to his homeland for several years. Although he tried hard to fit in with English society, he sorely missed the freedom and relaxed social atmosphere of western Canada.

Originally, in 1898, he had arrived in Canada as a remittance man, a person who receives generous financial support from his family in England.

A few remittance men were social outcasts who had been a source of embarrassment to their well-to-do families. Usually, they had been involved in mishandling funds or in getting familiar with a maid.

By far, most of the remittance men were outstanding British gentlemen of unblemished character. They first appeared after 1850 when it no longer became possible to purchase an army commission in Britain.

The "remittance man" became a product of an English land inheritance custom. When a wealthy land owner died, the entire estate would be inherited by the oldest son, in order to avoid dividing the estate into several inheritance units. Other sons were treated fairly by sending them to western Canada, and paying their way. At that time, Canada was anxious to settle the western provinces, and the remittance men were welcomed with open arms.

Each month, the displaced son would receive a generous remittance from home; hence, the name "remittance man". Most of these young men arrived in Canada to seek adventure and enjoy a sporting life in the wide-open spaces of the west. They did not come to Canada to do physical work. Many had sufficient financial resources to purchase ranches in southern Alberta, where they masqueraded as cowboys. They wore chaps, Stetsons, cowboy boots, spurs and a six-gun in a holster.

The remittance cowboy spent much of his time in the normal pursuits of an English gentleman, which centred on polo, cricket, hunting, fishing and carousing. Certainly not in more mundane ranching activities such as, fence-repairing, haying, branding and tending livestock.

Other significant contingents of remittance men congregated in Saskatchewan (Cannington Manor in the south-east), and in British Columbia at Wallashyn and near Duncan on Vancouver Island.

The Cannington Manor development started out very ambitiously, but eventually collapsed for lack of funds. The Wallashyn Settlement west of Kamloops was originally touted as an orchardist's paradise. Many varieties of fruit trees were planted and a very long wooden flume was constructed to supply irrigation water from the mountains. The flume was poorly designed and broke down repeatedly. This caused a lot of frustration. The First World War came to the rescue. Every able-bodied man joined up and Wallashyn was abandoned.

Before his arrival in Vegreville in 1927, John had already decided on his role in the community. He would become a weather man, an amateur meteorologist. He came equipped with appropriate instruments: a thermometer which registered both maximum and minimum temperatures, a barometer, a rain gauge and a weather vane.

He installed these instruments appropriately and began the task of preparing daily weather forecasts for the local citizenry. He maintained a rigid daily routine. Each morning after breakfast he would read his instruments and then compose a weather forecast for the day. He would use many layers of onion skin paper separated by carbon paper in his typewriter in order to produce many copies.

His appearance was in keeping with upper class standards. He always wore a clean white shirt and a tie from a renowned British school. His shirt sported a detachable collar and cuffs held in place by gold studs. He created the impression of a refined gentleman as he strutted down the street, clutching a folder containing weather forecasts in one hand and briskly swinging a fold-up black umbrella in the other.

He wore highly polished black oxford shoes and grey spats. His grey slacks were complemented by a navy blue blazer and a matching vest. A vest pocket held an expensive watch attached to a gold chain draped across his tummy. A gold watch fob embossed with his family crest added a classy touch to his appearance. To top it off, he wore a black bowler hat set squarely on his head.

He provided a daily weather forecast service to any business man who showed the least interest in his endeavors. He charged no fee. It was sufficient reward to socialize with his friends. He arranged his deliveries to fully occupy his day and suit his convenience.

Many of his clients gave him a polite reception, but little else. Others were more friendly and he spent much of his day in their places of business enjoying their conversation and their hospitality. At mid-morning he stopped in at the lumberyard for a cup of tea and a game of cribbage. At noon he would invariably drop in at Jim Chow's cafe and enjoy soup and a sandwich and plenty of gossip, depending on who else was there. He was always offered a cup of tea by the pharmacist, so he would arrange to be at the "chemists" around 3:00 p.m. At one of the grain elevators he would be supplied with a generous serving of illegally distilled moonshine mixed with 7Up. He would arrive there at 4:30 p.m. Sometimes this visit would extend to a second or third "prairie cocktail" and occasionally he would get an invitation to a delicious home cooked meal.

He stuck to this routine during the week; however, his clients' business establishments were closed on Sundays. He realized how critically important his daily forecasts were to the community, so on Sunday morning he would deliver them at the church door immediately after service. Fortunately, the two churches in town had services at different times enabling maximum distribution.

He fulfilled his meteorological role for many years, but one winter day he missed out on the forecast of a blizzard. It happened on the day that he had been invited to a Sunday dinner at a farm a half mile from town. As he left the town, the full fury of the blizzard suddenly struck and developed into a total white-out. He became confused and lost his way. His body was not found until three days later when the blizzard subsided.

It was the first and last time that he had erred in his forecast. According to a Vegreville resident, the remittance man's thermometers and barometer are still on display in the local Museum.

Kid Smarts

In 1928 my cousin Lou's father suffered a terrible accident on his farm near Humboldt, Saskatchewan. His father's torn jacket sleeve became entangled in the belt-drive of a wood-splitting machine. He received severe head injuries and could no longer function normally. He was confined to a mental institution.

At the time, Lou was seven years old. In the absence of their father, two older brothers aged thirteen and fifteen, took on the responsibility of managing the farm.

Despite his tender age, Lou gradually became aware that his family was having a hard time making ends meet. It was sort of a double whammy. Try as they may, his two older brothers could not completely fill the role of farm manager that their father had to give up. On top of that, crop failures and low crop prices had reduced farm income to a trickle.

One evening Lou overheard a conversation between his oldest brother, George, and his mother. Lou had fallen asleep on the couch right after supper, but he woke up suddenly when he heard his mother's voice become shrill and filled with emotion.

She was complaining to George, "I'm just not looking forward to Christmas this year. It's only two weeks away and I've done nothing to prepare for it. Usually by this time I would have made two or three types of candy, several batches of Christmas cookies and several real fruity Christmas cakes. We just don't seem to have the money to buy the ingredients."

Lou decided, then and there, that he would find some way to help earn the money his family needed.

The next summer, when Lou was helping his brothers bring in a load of hay from a distant field, he saw a full-grown weasel skipping about on a rock pile. A good part of their farm had consisted of very stony soil. Over the years their father had excavated stones and transported them to the field perimeters using a horse-drawn stone boat. There they were piled loosely in a fairly straight line.

Eventually, after years of toil, the boundaries of many fields were distinguished by rock piles two to three feet high. The gaps between the loosely-piled stones provided a haven for weasels, and this is where they nested. Their offspring were provided with safety and shelter.

Lou had heard that weasels were trapped for their pelts. He asked his brothers about this and was told that a weasel pelt could be sold for around one dollar. This sounded like a lot of money to Lou, and he decided that he would become a trapper to help out the family. Quite an adult decision for a boy about to celebrate his eighth birthday.

During the first winter of trapping Lou did not travel far from the beaten path. Their farm was three miles from school. In the winter they traveled to school in a caboose, a little hut with a wood stove, mounted on a horse-drawn sled. He set three gopher traps at rock piles located near the road, and checked them on the way home from school. Lou caught only two weasels that winter, but he received a dollar and seventy-five cents for the pelts and proudly gave the fur buyer's cheque to his mother.

During the second winter of trapping, Lou moved his trap line several times. His older brother had cautioned him against depleting the entire weasel population of a given area. By shifting his trap line frequently, he could preserve the breeding stock.

Around mid-winter, he decided to follow his brother's advice and shift his trapline to a new area. Little did he realize that in so doing he would be facing a life-threatening incident.

It was a Saskatchewan winter's day at its best. The air was crisp and cool, perhaps a few degrees below freezing. Certainly cold enough that Lou could see the vapour of his breath. Although the sky was mostly a clear transparent blue, there were a few dark clouds far to the north. Visibility was unlimited.

He approached a lengthy rock pile and began to search for likely places to set weasel traps. Although he became completely absorbed in his activities, he gradually became aware of a change in the weather. The sky was darkening, and he could now feel the wind on his cheek. He looked up. The clear, blue sky was rapidly being invaded by ugly, black clouds driven from the north.

As the storm gained momentum, the wind began to moan softly, and Lou's imagination caught fire. He stood still and listened carefully for a few moments. At first he thought he could hear faint wailing as if someone was in pain. It was the sound of wind, and it steadily increased in volume. He became frightened.

Lou began to think out loud. "I know for sure that I must not panic."

Then he took a close look at the problem. "Should I be worried about staying warm? I'm certainly wearing enough clothes: long johns, heavy woollen pants, a thick lumberjack shirt, a woollen vest, an old curling sweater of my dad's and a wind-proof jacket.

On top of that, I've got woollen socks, felt-lined boots , woollen mittens under leather mittens, as well as a home-knit toque."

He instinctively recognized that all this clothing offered little protection against sustained exposure to the storm. The wind was the real enemy. He must find shelter from it if he was to survive.

He looked around. There were only two visible landscape features, the long rock pile bordering the field, and a huge straw pile about a hundred feet away.

Without hesitation he ran over to the straw pile and sat down on the lee side. The wind exposure eased up considerably. When he looked back, he could no longer see the rock pile. The swirling snow had suddenly created a white-out. He felt terribly alone.

Again, he voiced his thoughts, "I have to make a decision, and very soon, before I get chilled to the bone."

There were few choices. He knew he should not leave and try to find his way home. No longer were there any landmarks. He could get lost in a few minutes. He would have to stay put, but he must get out of the storm. Then he had an idea. Maybe this straw pile was the answer.

"Why don't I dig a tunnel into the straw to get out of the wind?"

He did not wait to answer his own question. Instead, he fell to his knees and tried to pull out handfuls of straw. But there was a problem. The straw at the base of the pile was compressed and the surface was encrusted with ice crystals. Fortunately, he had a scout knife with a large blade. Using this tool he cut a square hole into the straw. He continued working as hard as he could, and soon the tunnel was several feet long. As he progressed, he pushed the loose straw behind him and completely blocked the tunnel entrance. The wind was no longer a threat. The tunnelling work had warmed him up, but now that it was finished, he lay there quietly, completely surrounded by straw as though he was sealed in a cocoon. The total darkness was just a little bit scary.

The sound of the wind was now muffled. However, he could still hear the rise and fall in volume, pitch and cadence. No doubt about it, this storm would rage all night.

Lou was tired as a result of his frenzied digging. He began to feel drowsy.

Before going to sleep, Lou started to think about his family. Would they be worried about him? Would they go out in the blinding blizzard to search for him?

He also thought about the hot meal now on the table at home. First thing this morning his mother had been chopping up vegetables for a beef stew, Lou's favourite dish.

Fortunately, sleep took over and killed his appetite.

Meanwhile, at home there was real concern. Lou's oldest brother was very upset.

"We can't go out looking for him in this weather. We'd get lost in the white-out. On top of that, I don't really know where to look."

That morning, Lou had told him about a new location for his trap line. Lou had said, "I'm taking your advice to heart. You know - you told me not to trap all the weasels in a particular area, but always to leave some breeding stock. So today I'm going to re-locate my trap line."

Their mother grudgingly agreed that they should not search for Lou in the blizzard. However, she felt compelled to do something.

"Boys, will you light a couple of coal oil lamps? Put them upstairs, one in the front window and the other one in the back window. You never know. The light just might catch his eye." Then she added, "Dad had a hockey referee's whistle. I think I'll take it outside and blow it as loud as I can. You never can tell. He could be within earshot."

She dressed warmly and opened the door. Before she could take a step outside a blast of wind caught her and nearly forced her back into the kitchen. She grabbed the door jamb, steadied herself and struggled outside.

She stayed there for a matter of seconds. Her effort was futile. The whistle could not be heard above the shrieking, howling wind.

As soon as Lou woke up the next morning, he started to back out of the tunnel. When he got near the entrance, he paused to listen. All was calm and quiet. He emerged into a clear, sunny morning. Not a breath of wind. He had no difficulty in establishing his bearings, and was soon on his way home.

Before dawn, Lou's older brothers started to prepare for a search. At daybreak, they mounted their horses and started riding in a southerly direction. They had covered only a half a mile when they saw someone walking in the distance. Without a doubt, it was their brother Lou. They watched as he broke his stride and began running toward them.

Lou was none the worse for having been caught in a blizzard. He insisted that he felt great, except for a terrible hunger. He had missed two meals and had walked a couple of miles on an empty stomach.

This event in Lou's life occurred nearly seventy years ago. I marvelled at the presence of mind and practicality of a nine-year-old who survived a terrible blizzard by remaining calm and using his head.

Saved by the Bells

This story was told to me by Harold McInnis who, with his wife Louva, lives happily on a quiet street in the James Bay district of Victoria.

Years ago, I worked as a parts man for a man named Jack who owned an automotive business in Lanigan (90 miles east of Saskatoon). He sold cars, trucks and tractors and owned several dealerships.

Jack had been invited to Regina to attend a demonstration of a new Lanz diesel tractor from Germany. He decided to drive his car to Regina to attend, and invited myself and a well-off farmer named Arthur, who was interested in buying a tractor, to go along with him. We left Lanigan around 8:00 a.m. on a bright, mild, sunny day in late February.

We reached Regina shortly after 10:00 a.m., had coffee, and then proceeded to the big machine shop where this novel tractor was on display. We spent around three hours discussing performance, maintenance and costs and then decided to have lunch with several old friends who had been at the demonstration.

The weather had warmed up considerably, so we decided to walk to a restaurant a few blocks away. It was almost like spring; there was even some meltwater flowing in the gutter by the curb. I began to wish I had worn a lighter coat.

The discussion after lunch went on and on and touched on many topics. Finally, at 4:00 p.m., we decided that it was time to return to Lanigan.

As we left the restaurant, it became apparent that our balmy weather had done an about-face and a fine powdery snow had begun to fall. I was a bit concerned as we left the outskirts of Regina and headed north. Prairie snow storms were nothing to take lightly. Sure enough, a half hour later it began snowing harder and a strong west wind suddenly sprang up.

As we drove along at a good clip, the weather continued to deteriorate. The wind intensified and there were now almost continuous clouds of snow swirling across the road, so much so that our visibility was impaired. Now it was dark too, and that added to our visibility problem. Jack was forced to reduce speed and I again began to feel uneasy. I suddenly realized that we had not seen another vehicle traveling on the road for at least twenty minutes. Had all the smart drivers already taken shelter?

As we approached the town of Raymore, I suggested to Jack that we stay over night in a hotel and wait out the bad weather in safety and comfort. Arthur agreed with me, but my boss snorted indignantly, "Are you guys crazy? Why spend money on a hotel room when we are only a few miles from home? These are just little snow squalls. You know that we seldom get a severe blizzard this late in February."

I certainly did not agree with him, but I bit my lip, wrestled with my conscience, and kept quiet; he was, after all, the boss, and maybe we would be alright if we carried on.

Less than ten miles after leaving Raymore, we suddenly came to a dead halt in a snowbank. It happened in a place where the road was located in a deep cut at least four feet below the adjacent fields. This cut was choked with drifts of hard-packed wind-blown powder snow and we were inextricably stuck. Jack turned off the engine and all was silent inside the car. An eerie feeling pervaded. Outside in the darkness the wind was howling and screaming. There was nothing to see out there. Could it possibly get any worse?

Jack turned the motor back on to keep the heater going while we took stock of the situation. To stay in the car would mean shelter for a while, but when the fuel ran out and the heater quit it wouldn't be long before we would freeze. By then, the drifts would be deeper as the blizzard continued. Conversely, leaving the car to stumble through the darkness could also lead to getting lost and not being found until spring. However, with luck, and managing to stay between the fences on either side of the road, we might just make it to a farm house before we froze. Damn Jack for not listening to us and stopping in Raymore for the night!

Leaving the car would give us only slightly better survival odds. And that was good enough for me. I decided that I would leave the car, alone if necessary. That decision was reinforced by the thought of my wife Louva and four children waiting for me. My livelihood was their livelihood. Fortunately Arthur had come to the same decision as I; we were both convinced that it would be suicidal to remain in the car.

Jack thought otherwise. In a loud voice he warned us, "Don't you guys realize that this is a total white-out? You'll be lost in two minutes. We're probably only ten or twelve miles from Lanigan. Why take such a risk?"

This was indeed a sobering thought, but I still disagreed with him, and this time I spoke up. "If we stay in the car we'll freeze to death as soon as the motor conks out."

I was certain that this would happen, either because we would eventually run out of gas or because the exhaust pipe would get completely plugged up by drifting snow. Arthur and I bundled up as best we could. Fortunately we both had warm mittens and winter caps with ear flaps. I was now very grateful for my heavy, warm, winter coat.

The drifting snow had already accumulated so much that we had difficulty opening the car door to get out. As we stepped out we were immediately blasted full force by the wind which took my breath away. I was almost tempted to re-enter the car.

Other than this fierce wind, our most immediate problem was visibility. We could only see a couple of feet ahead. To avoid losing contact with one another, we strung a scarf between us and clutched the ends tightly.

We had decided to find the fence and then follow it, hopefully to a farm house. The adjacent fields, being on higher ground, had only a very shallow covering of snow. Our struggle from the car to the field was almost comic had the situation not been so serious. We fell several times where there were pockets of soft snow between snowbanks. We hung onto the scarf and, in about ten minutes, we scrambled to a field. The fence ran parallel to the road. We were trying to decide in which direction we should follow the fence, when suddenly we heard a sound.

The wind had faltered and faded, dying down to a mere whisper. During this momentary lull, we heard, briefly, a strange metallic ringing. It most certainly was not a blizzard sound. It sounded like it had come from our left, near the fence line.

We stood absolutely still in the swirling snow, our bodies tensed, concentrating our hearing off to the left. Our mouths were open and our eyes strained to see through the driving snow, but the wind picked up again and the sound was gone.

Suddenly, there was another lull in the storm. The wind stopped howling and again we heard the strange sound, this time closer and more distinct. Amazingly, it sounded like the jingling of sleigh bells. You know. The little Christmas bells festooned on the horses' harnesses in winter.

As we strained to listen, the sound became continuous. The bells were getting closer. We grabbed each others shoulders and did a little dance in the snow.

Out of the swirling storm the snowy forms of two black horses emerged, pulling a sleigh with a long grain box. For protection from the wind, two heavily-blanketed men were hunkered down so deeply in the box that they were barely visible to Arthur and me. The rig took on a ghostly appearance: just two Christmas-belled horses and a phantom sleigh bearing down on us through this terrible blizzard

There were two bachelor brothers, Dick and Art, in the sleigh returning to their farm from town where they had picked up their mail and some supplies. They, too, had been caught in this blizzard, and they were following the fence to find their way home.

Through the snowy haze they suddenly spotted two equally-ghostly figures dancing in the snow near the fence.

Dick turned to Art: "Do you see what I see?"

Art was still too shocked by this strange apparition. He could not believe his eyes. There really were two cumbersome figures cavorting in the snow during a blizzard in the middle of nowhere.

Art stammered, "I guess we should stop and find out what they are up to. Something very strange, I'll bet."

By this time, the dancing had ceased and Arthur and I were now wildly waving our arms and yelling as loud as we could.

The ghostly rig and its passengers merged into reality as they halted a few feet from us. We were so excited that we both tried to talk at the same time to tell them of our plight.

Dick shouted, "Save the details for later! Just get aboard and we'll make tracks."

First, Arthur and I had to plough our way back to the car to rescue Jack. Luckily, the wind had not completely obliterated our tracks or we might not have found the car. We kicked away a lot of snow in order to open the car door. The engine had already conked out, and Jack was shivering uncontrollably . We pulled him out of the car, and hustled him to the waiting sleigh. There were several blankets in the sleigh to bundle up in and the horses resumed their homeward-bound journey, bells tinkling merrily in the blowing snow.

When we arrived at their farm, Dave unhitched and took care of the horses while Art led the way to the house. We were chilled to the bone and could hardly wait to get a fire going. While we waited for the wood stove to heat up, I tried to phone my wife, but the storm had taken out the phone lines. I could picture her waiting and worrying about me.

The blizzard worsened. The brothers strung a rope from the house to the barn so they would not get lost while tending to the livestock. We huddled in the little house all night with the wind whistling through the cracks in the west wall, and leaking out through similar cracks in the east wall, taking a generous amount of the heat with it. Fortunately, there was a big supply of dry white poplar firewood.

We discovered that Dave and Art had a very limited supply of food: coffee, canned milk, bread, butter and baloney! That's what they served the first night as well as for every other meal for the next three days.

Toward evening on the second day, telephone service was restored and I phoned home. Louva tried to maintain a calm and composed voice, but I could tell from a slight tremor that she was concerned. It was a comfort for me to hear the children in the background. I told her that I would return home as soon as the weather permitted.

The morning of the fourth day dawned in an aura of optimism. There was not a breath of wind. It was serene and sunny. The temperature hovered around freezing. We could again take to the road.

Art and Dave agreed to help rescue our car from the snow drift and we set off in the sleigh with several shovels. The car was not visible, but after a few minutes we did locate it and started digging. When it was finally freed, we thanked the two brothers profusely.

Just before we drove away, Jack pressed two twenty-dollar bills into Dave's hand and in an emotional voice just above a whisper he said, "Thanks so much. You saved our lives."

Total silence prevailed in the car during our return trip to Lanigan. Each of us was wrapped up in his own thoughts and feelings. I had no idea what Jack was thinking but I felt sure that Arthur shared my thoughts about the predicament we had survived. I truly believed that Jack had endangered our lives by refusing to stop over in Raymore.

Although I felt like telling him what I really thought, I simply could not get up the nerve to do so. After all, he was my boss. Jobs were hard to find. I was married with a family. I could well lose my job if I said what I thought.

On the other hand, Arthur was not an employee. As the car came to a stop in Lanigan, Arthur stepped out. Before closing the door on the passenger side of the car, he leaned forward, took a deep breath, and thrust a forefinger within an inch of Jack's face. He then spit out these words of accusation.

"Jack, I've known you for many years, and I always thought well of you. It took a life-threatening blizzard to show me what kind of a man you really are. You placed our lives in jeopardy by forcing your decision on us. I have promised myself to have nothing to do with you from here on."

Arthur slammed the door and walked away.

While this was taking place, I got out of the back seat, silently thanking Arthur for saying what I dared not, and muttered a brief good-bye. I quickly walked home, anxious to return to the love and warmth of my family.

I never did see Dave or Art again, and I can't even recall their surname, but over the years, whenever I see baloney on display in a deli, I fondly remember them and have to smile.

The Totzke Blizzard

Were the prairie blizzards of the Great Depression really more fierce and life-threatening than they are now? My sister Lucille believes they were. Perhaps you would too if you had shared her experiences on a winter trip from Saskatoon to our home in Cudworth.

Here is her story as she told it to me.

Being the oldest child in the family, I was also the first to fly the nest. I had just finished a year (1939/40) of business school training at the Sprott Shaw School in Saskatoon, and I was undertaking my first job-hunting activity. The Civil Service examinations were slated for early December in Saskatoon, and despite stormy weather I managed to get there on time traveling by train from Cudworth.

The exam was right on target with my training. As soon as I finished writing it I experienced that inner glow that told me I had done exceedingly well. Before returning to Cudworth, I stayed over night with relatives in Saskatoon. The next morning I hustled over to the CNR station to catch a train going cast on the main line. After about forty-five minutes on this train, I would have to switch to a branch line at Totzke for a half hour trip to Cudworth.

At the railway station the temperature was well below zero, but worst of all was the wind. The snow was swirling around and drifting as I boarded the train. Although I had been outside for only a few minutes, I was chilled to the bone. I began to feel a premonition that I could be in for a rough time. Perhaps I should have worn another sweater and brought warmer gloves.

The mainline east of Saskatoon had plenty of traffic and was clear of snow, so we arrived at Totzke on time. Best news of all, our train to Cudworth was waiting at the station. There was only a handful of passengers who occupied the day coach: one elderly couple, and three of us in our late teens. We settled ourselves as comfortably as possible and awaited the start of our journey. By this time, the wind was howling and moaning. Occasionally it would scream as it vibrated the overhead telegraph wires. Visibility was so reduced we could barely see the railway station. Our small group of young people chatted noisily as we made acquaintances. I noticed that the old couple was silent and appeared worried.

Suddenly the engine tooted, a bell rang and the train slowly inched forward. Unbeknownst to the engineer, the railway line was plugged by snow drifts a few feet ahead. To increase traction the engineer released sand on the track, but he could get no momentum. Within minutes, the train was truly stuck in a huge snow bank.

In a few minutes, the conductor entered the coach with the news. "This day coach has no heat and no food, and we have no idea how long we will be stuck."

Although the weather had now reached blizzard conditions, the conductor recommended that the younger passengers should attempt to scramble through about one hundred feet of snowdrifts to the warmth of the Totzke railway station.

The younger passengers groaned loudly when they looked out the window. The old couple trembled and tightly clutched the heavy blanket that the conductor had just given to them.

I was already shivering with the cold, so I did not hesitate. I clambered down the steps of the coach, and then had to jump into waist deep snow. The station lights glimmered weakly through the snowy haze. In less than five tiring minutes, I found myself in a warm room with friendly people and hot food and drinks. After the meal, we settled ourselves as comfortably as possible and waited for a snowplough to rescue our little train. I noticed that the train crew (three people) had entered the station a few minutes after us, but somehow I had lost track of the old couple.

The benches in the small waiting room of the station were not designed for comfort. All of us slept on the floor. When I woke up the next morning, my muscles felt stiff and sore. A cup of steaming coffee helped me to recover.

Gradually, the dawn absorbed the darkness and I went to the window to look outside. There were huge drifts of snow as far as the eye could see. The sky was clear. Not a cloud in sight. Not even a breath of wind. We had seen the last of yesterday's blizzard.

Suddenly, I heard the muted sound of a locomotive whistle far off in the distance. Could this be the snowplough from Prince Albert coming to our rescue? I threw on my coat and rushed outside onto the station platform. In the distance I could barely distinguish the snowplough. Its progress was marked by a spiralling column of black smoke from the locomotive which pushed it along the track. A few minutes later, the red snowplough became clearly visible, the immense V-blade nearly dwarfing the locomotive.

Whenever the plough split a snow drift, it flung a huge plume of snow towering far out to either side of the railway.

The station platform trembled violently as this gigantic unit thundered and hissed up to the station. Just before screeching to a halt, the engineer gave a little toot on the whistle. I heard him tell the station agent that the railway track was now clear all the way to Prince Albert. He explained that the snowplough had been purposefully delayed to allow the blizzard to blow itself out and make snowploughing practical.

We soon boarded our train. In a few minutes we chugged out of Totzke with bell clanging and whistle blowing to announce our departure.

We were only a few miles from Cudworth when a cold chill gave me the shivers, almost violently. I had a strong feeling that something was really wrong, and I immediately realized what it was.

I turned my head and looked at all the other passengers. There was no sign of the elderly couple who had remained on the train. at Totzke. Before I could discuss this with anyone else, our train came to a stop in Cudworth, and in the excitement of homecoming it slipped my mind.

For several days after the blizzard I checked the Saskatoon Star Phoenix - but not a word appeared about the Totzke blizzard. I found myself vaguely speculating whether an old couple's bones would some day appear from under a giant snow bank. Perhaps some friends had met the old couple in Totzke. I suppose I'll never really know what happened to them.

Incidentally, I did pass my exams with flying colours, and two weeks later I was busy in a brand new job in Regina.

Part VII

OPPORTUNITY KNOCKS

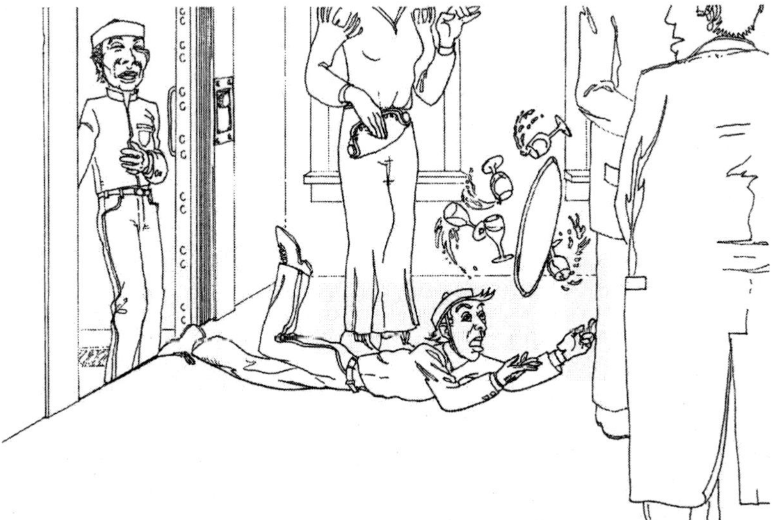

I could well have named this chapter "The Light at the End of the Tunnel".

For many prairie people caught in the grip of the Depression there was very little light and the tunnel was endless. Although some folks were able to find steady employment in the prairie provinces, the wages were very low. Many people had to travel elsewhere in Canada to find a future. For a larger number of young men, the Depression ended when they joined Canada's armed forces during World War II.

It is a sad reflection on our society that it took a major war which killed millions of people to provide economic opportunity and break the tyranny of the Depression. Thousands of young westerners flocked to the recruiting centres.

Surprisingly enough, many chose to join the Navy - even though practically none of them had ever seen the sea. I think that joining the Navy was a built-in reaction to get as far away as possible from drought and dust storms.

"North Atlantic Holiday" is the story of a young Saskatchewan man who faced the very worst challenges that the North Atlantic had to offer. Yet, he was one of those who found opportunity for a new life in Canada's armed forces.

A Broken Bike and a Baby Pig

Lou's teen-age brother ran into the house and spilled the bad news to nine-year-old Lou.

"When Uncle George left just a few minutes ago, he backed his car right over your bike lying in the yard, and completely wrecked it. Then he drove off as though he had not even noticed."

Lou scrambled to his feet and ran outside. He realized that he had been careless, leaving his bike on the ground near the milking yard, after bringing in the cows from the pasture. He glumly looked down at the broken remains of his bike, and burst into tears.

Two years ago, this bike had been resurrected from the town dump. Lou's older brother had worked long and hard to restore it to running condition. Now it was useless. No longer would he be able to bike out to the pasture to bring the cows home for milking. Nor would he be able to ride to and from the little country school.

This was not the only bad news for Lou on that particular day.

When school had ended that spring, Lou's mother had laid down the law. "Lou, now that summer holidays have begun, it will be your job to keep the neighbour's pigs out of our garden. Everyone else in this family has a job to do, and now you've got one, too."

Lou had no love for this family of pigs that posed a threat to the garden. A big, fat Tamworth sow led the invasion, followed by her family of twelve little piglets. They would attack his mother's prize vegetables and root up the soil almost anywhere in the garden. Chasing these animals out of the garden and down the road to the neighbour's farm was not Lou's idea of fun.

Lou brought the wheelbarrow from the tool shed and sadly loaded the remains of his bike to take them to the junk pile beyond the barn. As he was just completing the job, he heard his mom yell for him.

"Lou, the pigs are headed for the garden again. You better chase them away!"

Lou did not answer immediately.

"Lou, will you answer me? Those darn pigs have got to go before they cause damage!"

"Yeah, Mom, I heard you."

Lou picked up a stick and trotted toward the garden. While he attended to his job, he collected his thoughts.

"What can I do about my situation? I no longer have a bike. Nor is there any money to buy one. And I've got this awful job of chasing pigs."

Several ideas ran through his mind and, suddenly, he got an inspiration.

The neighbour's pigs were Tamworths, the same breed as the ones on Lou's farm. Both farms supported piglets of the same age and size. It would be impossible to tell them apart.

Lou pondered, "Just maybe I could get away with taking one of these pigs and transferring it securely in our pig barn with our piglets."

No one was looking. Lou quickly grabbed a baby pig by the hind legs and deposited the pig in the pig barn. So far, so good!

The neighbour's pigs did not appear at the garden that week, nor the next.

Lou thought, "Maybe the neighbours have mended their pig pen."

Meanwhile, Lou's "pilfered pig", which he affectionately called Tammy, ate just like a pig is supposed to, and grew to mature market size in a hurry, along with others of the same age. In the fall, a half dozen pigs were sold, including Tammy, and he collected fourteen dollars for his "adopted" porker.

The next day Lou walked three miles to Humboldt and visited a hardware store. He told the owner that he had fourteen dollars and wanted to buy a bike. The storekeeper considered the matter for a moment or two, glanced at Lou's worn-out shoes and patched clothing , and replied, "I think we have a bike on sale for exactly that amount."

In a few minutes, Lou was pedalling home with a broad grin on his face.

For a while Lou thought that perhaps he might not get away with the "pig for a bike" deal. However, he rationalized that his action was not really theft since the neighbour's pigs had enjoyed a good many free meals in the garden. Lou still remained a little bit uneasy, and occasionally, he would have a dream of a Mountie knocking on his door with a stern look on his face and a summons in his hand.

Lou's new bike was certainly built to last. For many years its performance was first rate, whether on the bumpy, stony pasture lands on the farm, or on the daunting highways and byways of Saskatchewan.

His attachment to the bike was suddenly terminated by the onset of World War II. He left the farm to join the army. Just before leaving, he carefully stored the bike at the rear of the tool shed.

When the war ended six years later, Lou returned home briefly.

He never even gave a thought to the bike or to the nefarious tactics used to acquire it.

Through Adversity to the Stars

When twenty year-old Bill Johnstone first set foot on Canadian soil on May 22, 1928, he was full of hope for a bright future in a new land. He had laboured as a coal miner in northern England since his thirteenth birthday. From now on he would not be toiling underground in unhealthy and unsafe conditions. He remembered too well working long hours with a pick and shovel while in a crouched or kneeling position. He also recalled hearing the creak of overstrained timbers and pit props, sometimes wondering if a major rock failure would overwhelm him. He was eagerly looking forward to a healthy outdoor life in the clean air and open spaces of western Canada.

After having experienced a "sea sick" Atlantic crossing, Bill traveled by rail to Winnipeg where he arrived in good physical and mental shape. He was then instructed to continue by train to Holden, Alberta, where he was hired to work on a farm for twenty dollars a month plus board.

Little did Bill realize that he would endure over five years of hard work and hardship in Alberta, and also return to coal mining, before his life would stabilize at a satisfactory level.

During those early days on the farm he encountered one new experience after another. Bill adapted readily to his new life and soon learned to harness horses, milk cows, care for many types of livestock, clean barns and operate farm machinery. He applied himself diligently to every chore that came his way. As a result, the farmer was very much impressed with this "ex-coal miner", and at the end of the first month he raised Bill's wages to thirty dollars per month, a substantial fifty percent increase. During harvest time his pay was increased threefold.

The farmer had no work for him during the winter, so Bill looked around for a job in the mining industry. He soon found work in a lignite coal mine near Camrose, Alberta.

In early 1929 he got word from England that his father and mother plus six siblings had applied to emigrate to Canada under a land settlement scheme. Work at the mine discontinued in March 1929. A few weeks later his family arrived in Vermilion, Alberta.

Very few positive statements could be made about the land on which they settled. It was located nine miles from the nearest community (nearly two hours' drive with a team of horses). This shocked Bill's mother who had been accustomed to shopping daily for fresh food in England. The nearest neighbour was half a mile away. This was even a bigger shock to her. She dearly missed afternoon tea with close neighbours. The soil was coarse textured and very stony, with a very low potential for tilled crops. At best it could be used as pasturage. It soon became apparent that they would not need a Depression, or drought or frost or hail to go broke on this land. Moreover, clearing and ploughing the land with primitive equipment was slow and laborious. It truly became a hardscrabble farm where output always fell short of input.

Altogether, Bill spent nearly ten years in Alberta trying desperately to make a decent living in both farming and mining. After reading his autobiography "Coal Dust in My Blood" I came to the conclusion that two particular years during the Depression could claim the distinction of being the most wretched periods of his life in Canada.

The first of this was the winter of 1929/30. This was the very first Canadian winter following his parents' immigration, and it proved to be a severe test of their determination and endurance. In that year they had managed to clear five acres of the one hundred and sixty acre farm, and plant a crop of oats, intended to provide winter food for the livestock. The summer had been dry, and poor crop yields were realized throughout the district. Bill could find no harvesting jobs in the vicinity so he traveled to Outlook, Saskatchewan where he managed to earn over two hundred dollars stooking and pitching bundles.

Bill's harvest earnings provided warm clothing and footwear for his siblings who attended school, as well as food and other essentials. When Christmas arrived, the money had all been spent and food supplies were low. The family relied upon easily snared snow shoe rabbits for a meat supply. In his book Bill described their plight when he said, "We had reached the stage where there were more meal times than meals."

The second despondent period for Bill was from mid-1931 to mid-1932. He was plagued with bad luck for a whole year. In June 1931, while working in a coal mine, he was almost completely buried by falling rock from a mine cave-in. Fortunately, he did not suffer any broken bones but he had serious damage to ligaments and muscles. While convalescing he suffered acute appendicitis and required surgery. Although he had not completely recovered, the family was desperate for money so Bill went harvesting.

That fall an early frost caused heavy damage to their crop. The grade of wheat was lowered, and his father was paid only twelve cents a bushel.

A week before Christmas the whole family worked hard to prepare fifty turkeys for market. Bill was terribly disappointed when the buyer from Pat Burns graded the birds severely. Bill was offered a top price of eight cents a pound for high quality birds, and only six cents a pound for birds with a minor defect or those over twelve pounds in weight. Bill sold thirty-five birds for less than a dollar each. He refused to accept a lower price for the remaining fifteen birds. After returning them to the farm, they were frozen and eventually consumed by the family that winter.

Early in the new year, Bill searched far and wide for a mining job, but none could be found. Finally, he accepted a farm job as a "hired man" for which he was paid five dollars a month plus room and board.

When spring arrived, the family was short of food, so Bill's father applied for relief. Before being given a food voucher for twenty dollars, he had to clear brush and trees from a rural road right-of -way. Each year it was becoming more apparent that the farm was hopeless.

Bill finally got a break in 1934. He got a job as a coal miner near Wapamum, west of Edmonton. After several months of steady work, the job appeared to be secure and Bill decided to turn his back on farming forever. He would put down his roots in a mining community. He bought a building lot in Wapamum and built a house. He participated in community life, playing the piano in a dance orchestra, building a community tennis court and joining a soccer team. He also enrolled in a correspondence course to increase his knowledge of mining.

When Bill met an attractive young lady named Dorothy Riddock, he became convinced that his life had indeed taken a favorable turn. They soon recognized in each other the ability to adapt to negative circumstances. Bill had been severely tested by hardships imposed by the Depression. Dorothy had survived years of slaving on a farm under the harsh rule of an autocratic and ungrateful father.

It did not take long for them to realize that a shared life would be the best of good fortune and happiness for both of them. They still maintain this view after over sixty years of marriage.

When mine work slowed down to two days per week in 1937, Bill and his wife began exploring job opportunities elsewhere. They heard of coal mining expansion at Cumberland on Vancouver Island. Because of Bill's varied experience and knowledge, he was hired immediately. At first he worked underground as a miner, but gradually he was given more responsibility. Finally, in July 1952, he was promoted to the district superintendent position, responsible for the operation of the entire Cumberland mines.

Bill is now ninety-five years old, still with a clear memory and talent for creative writing.

I think the most appropriate expression which reflects the lives of this couple is the R.C.A.F. motto, *per ardua ad astra* (through adversity to the stars). Both Bill and Dorothy have experienced much adversity but after sixty-four years of marriage, they still have stars in their eyes.

Hair Red Like Sunset

As she busied herself in the semi-darkness of the sod house, Georgina recalled her earliest days at this remote Saskatchewan homestead.

As a newly-wed she had arrived after a long, uncomfortable ride in a horse-drawn wagon. When she and her brand new husband had stopped in front of the strange-looking farm house, she had taken a long exploratory look, and said to herself, "What a desolate, ugly, uninspiring place to call home! If I had wings I would leave right now."

But she could not face the punishment of the three hour wagon ride back to town. Nearly every muscle and bone in her body ached and complained.

In almost a whisper she answered her husband's questioning look. "I guess I'll have to take a good look at the place."

Bill took her hand and helped her to get down from the wagon.

It was not an impressive entry into the hut. The door had stuck, and Bill had to give a sharp pull to open it. When Georgina stepped inside she was almost overcome by the dank smell and the gloom. The place had never experienced a drop of paint, inside or out. There was only one door and just a few small windows. The tears began to flow. An immediate return trip to town began to look appealing.

She had despaired. "Could I ever possibly make this place my home?"

Somehow she had stuck it out, and now two years later, she was reasonably happy, especially since the arrival of her cute little red-headed baby boy whom everyone called Red. Homestead life had become a lot less lonely.

One morning in early spring, she had already fed and changed her infant when she was distracted by a noise outside. She glanced out the window and saw a man astride a small bay pony. She opened the door and went outside. On closer examination, she saw that the rider was an Indian, probably a Sioux from west of their farming community.

He spoke quietly in a monotone. "I got two wagon loads fence posts to sell. Maybe your man buy from me?"

She replied, " My husband left right after breakfast to haul water from a neighbour's well. He should be back very soon."

The Indian showed no emotion. He shrugged his shoulders and muttered, " I wait."

She nodded and re-entered the house to continue her house work. Some time later, she glanced outside and noticed that the Indian still sat motionless on his horse. She also noted that the sun was well up in the sky and that there was no wind. Maybe it was a good time to put the baby outside to get some fresh air.

She brought out the cradle and placed it in a sunny spot against the wall of the house. When she brought out the baby, she cuddled him closely. His real name was Bill, but no one used that name because his head displayed a bountiful thatch of bright red, curly hair. So everyone called him Red.

Although the Indian remained motionless on his horse while Georgina moved around, his eyes followed every move she made. When he first spied the exposed red hair, his eyes opened wide and he gave an almost inaudible gasp of surprise.

Georgina tucked in the baby and then re-entered the house. Very quietly the Indian slowly dismounted, and with a quick glance toward the door, he stealthily approached the cradle. He bent over the baby and gently moved the blanket a few inches to gain an unobstructed view of Red's head. He was completely fascinated by the curly, red hair. He had never seen anything like it.

Meanwhile, Georgina had started to wash the breakfast dishes. She heard a slight noise and quickly glanced outside. She was very surprised to see the pony's empty saddle . Immediately, she became concerned.

"I wonder where he went." she thought. She dropped the dish towel and rushed to the window to get a wider view.

A few years before, when she first had arrived in Saskatchewan from Scotland, she had heard some unpleasant stories about natives, but until now she hadn't given them much thought.

It was not unusual for Georgina to be on her own with her baby. Her husband often worked in the fields on one job or another. Nevertheless, she began to feel a little bit uneasy . Perhaps it had not been wise of her to admit to their visitor that she was home alone.

She saw the Indian bending over the baby. She felt sudden apprehension when his hand reached out and moved the blanket away from the baby's head.

"What in the world is he doing!"

Then she saw the gentle smile crease his weather-beaten face and the kindness in his eyes, and she took a deep breath and totally relaxed.

Out she went, and joined him. The Indian had become completely enraptured by the baby's hair, and he did not notice that Georgina had joined him until she spoke softly. "Isn't he a beautiful child?"

With a glint of humour in his eyes, he asked her, "If you have babe for sale I'll trade you plenty. Four wagon loads of fence posts, or three horses."

He bent over again to get another close look at the baby. "Very nice hair. Maybe I trade you both horses and fence posts?"

Georgina was in the process of assuring him that her son was definitely not for sale, when her husband returned. She explained to him what had taken place. All three adults enjoyed a good chuckle.

After Bill and the Indian had come to an agreement about the purchase of some fence posts, the Indian again approached the cradle. After another admiring examination of the baby, he mounted his pony and said, "Plenty nice baby with hair like red sunset."

As the Indian rode away, Georgina realized she had just weathered another "first" in her on-going experiences in this strange land. This never would have happened back in Scotland.

North Atlantic Holiday

The Great Depression often forced the children of "needy" families to take on adult responsibilities. For Bob White, the process of becoming a farmer began soon after he started to attend school.

At nine years of age, Bob did most of the milking, usually three or four cows at 5:00 a.m. and the same number at 6:00 p.m. He already could drive different horse-drawn equipment. He used an axe to split firewood, and hunted game with a .22 rifle. At age fourteen he quit school and became a full time farmer.

The White family lived on a farm near Bodmin, Saskatchewan, eighty miles north-west of Prince Albert. There were only two children in the family, Bob and his sister Jean..

Bob's life on the farm had few happy or rewarding moments. There always seemed to be a struggle, just to make a living. He had learned to regard hardships, disappointments and misfortune as attributes of a normal life.

Eventually, farm life failed the White family. The final straw was the loss of their livestock in 1941. The horses died of some strange disease. The cattle were poisoned by an elderly deranged neighbour.

Bob's father left the farm to find a sawmill job in BC. Bob joined the Royal Canadian Navy and discovered that there were actually some aspects of life which could be enjoyed.

Bob told me several stories which have much to say about his character, his upbringing and the times in which he grew up.

* * *

One morning when Bob was fourteen, he woke up with a fiercely throbbing toothache. With tears in his eyes, he approached his dad, "I feel just terrible. Will you take a look in my mouth and see if you can help me?"

His dad examined the sore area. The adjacent gums were bright red and swollen. He applied pressure with his finger. Bob nearly passed out from the pain. The pressure produced a bead of yellow pus.

His dad suggested, "Bob, we're going to have to get this tooth pulled as soon as we can."

The nearest dentist was in Prince Albert, so Bob's dad decided to extract it himself. He selected a pair of pliers from his tool box and placed them in boiling water. When the pliers had cooled off, he got to work. With some difficulty he got a grip on the infected tooth, but the pliers slipped off as soon as he applied pressure. This added to the pain, and Bob was in agony. His face was contorted with pain and he could not hide his sobs. His dad tried twice more to extract the tooth, but still no luck.

"Bob, I just can't pull it. These pliers weren't designed to pull teeth. We're going to have to send you to Prince Albert somehow."

This decision presented a big problem. Where would they find the money to pay for rail transport to P.A. and for the dentist's fee? His father's pockets were empty. There was one last resort. His mother kept a little jar in the kitchen cupboard in which she saved loose change. She saved a nickel here and a dime there so that she could buy a few "extras" at Christmas. The change in this jar added up to two dollars and ten cents. Would this cover the dentist's fee?

They would still have to find a way to send him to P.A.. Randy, a twenty-five year old neighbour's son, had often ridden the freight trains illegally to travel to P.A. and even more distant communities. When told about the situation, he volunteered to accompany Bob on a freight train, and introduce him to hobo life.

Despite the pain, Bob became excited at the prospect of riding a freight train such a great distance. Up to this point in his life he had not traveled more than ten miles from his home.

First thing the next morning the two of them clambered aboard an outgoing freight train as it was leaving Big River. It was a warm morning, and despite his sore mouth, Bob began to enjoy the view of the countryside from the top of a boxcar. Randy chose to stay between two cars. Suddenly, a brakeman appeared on top of the train and approached. Bob panicked, and ran the other way. When he reached the last boxcar, he climbed partway down a ladder, with the intention of jumping from the train. He now realized that the train was moving at too high a speed. If he jumped now he would be severely injured, maybe fatally.

He looked up and saw the brakeman above him, yelling loudly.

"Go ahead and jump, young fellow. You know you're not allowed on this train."

He then stepped on Bob's fingers which grasped the ladder. Bob quickly moved his hands to a lower rung and pleaded with the brakeman.

"I'm afraid I'll kill myself if I jump here. Please let me stay until we stop at the next station."

The train man paused for a moment, and then agreed. "Make sure you get off at Canwood, or you'll be in big trouble."

Bob spent most of his money on train fare from Canwood to Prince Albert. By the time he arrived in that city he wasn't sure which hurt more: his abscessed tooth or his crushed fingers.

When he told the dentist about his misfortunes on the freight train, the dentist assured him that his tooth problem would be alleviated whether he got paid or not. In the end the dentist lent him enough money to pay his train fare back to Big River.

* * *

The first major test of Bob's maturity and physical endurance occurred when he was seventeen. A fisherman from Big River needed a helper for a winter fishing expedition at Dog Lake, about three days travel from Big River. They traveled the distance with horses and sleighs loaded with thousands of feet of fish net, fish boxes, food, and kerosene, as well as all the tools and equipment needed for their work and for cabin life.

The road was in terrible condition, just a track which meandered through the brush and across muskegs. The latter were treacherous because in places with deep snow, the muskeg had not yet frozen completely and could not support the weight of the horses. The horses broke through a couple of times and barely managed to regain their footing on solid ground.

Upon arrival at their destination, they discovered that the chinking had disappeared from between the logs of the cabin. Their first job was to "chink" up these gaps using snow splattered with water. This mixture froze immediately. After a few vigorous hours, they succeeded in making the cabin tight enough for habitation. There was no dry wood available. They did find a few dead trees to use for kindling, but living trees were to be the principle fuel. This green wood was difficult to burn and did not produce a desirable amount of heat.

Net fishing on the frozen lake was a punishing experience. They were exposed to the sweep of the north wind which often prevailed. The term "wind chill" was not yet in vogue, but Bob could certainly describe it. He used woolen mittens when handling the ice cold wet nets. Within a few minutes the mittens would be encrusted with ice. Every day he would use many pairs of mittens which would have to be thawed out and dried at night in the cabin.

After only one week of introductory work, Bob was forced to work alone. His partner had become seriously ill and was transported to Big River by Indians using a dog team and toboggan. It was the first time in his life that Bob was totally out of contact with another human being for several weeks. During the day his mind was fully occupied with the strenuous work on the lake. However, at night he became very lonely and even a bit homesick, especially when he heard the prolonged howling of a wolf pack.

* * *

After his father left the farm for a sawmill job in B.C. Bob moved to Prince Albert where he tried several different lines of work. His last job there was at the Pat Burns meat packing plant. He discovered that he could not tolerate the sounds and smells that went with the job. He was especially horrified by the gruesome shrieking of pigs in their last throes of life as they were knifed in the throat.

After much consideration, Bob decided to leave civilian life and try out a military career. He was attracted by the thought of adventure and travel. The time had come to leave Saskatchewan. In December of 1942 he joined the Royal Canadian Navy.

Bob's very first posting was to H.M.C.S. Naden in Victoria, where he took a cooking course.

Immediately upon completion of the course, he was shipped to Halifax and posted to a corvette which left port on convoy duty in the North Atlantic. A violent storm developed on the very first trip. The waves were immense and at times it looked as though the ship would founder. The effect of the storm upon the crew was devastating, and only a few escaped sea sickness.

Bob was one of the exceptions. In fact, the storm seemed to have an exhilarating effect on him. He developed a good set of "sea legs" by noon of the first day of the storm. He never lost his appetite. In some ways the ferocity of the storm reminded him of the icy north winds on the boreal forest lakes of Saskatchewan during his ice-fishing experience.

His first voyage in the navy began to take on the character of an adventure.

At the height of the storm the captain sent a message to the galley requesting sandwiches and coffee. At the time, Bob was the only kitchen staff member on duty. He prepared the order and delivered it to the bridge himself. Despite the violent rolling and pitching of the ship, he somehow managed to make his way from galley to the bridge without spilling any coffee. Upon entering the bridge he carefully placed the tray on a table. Wearing a broad smile on his face, he turned to the captain and said, "Here's your lunch, sir. Enjoy."

Up to this point in the day, the captain had not seen a smile on the face of any staff member. He was impressed with Bob's apparent cheerfulness, and decided to chat with him.

"Well, sailor, you seem to be weathering this storm like an old salt. How many trips have you made across the North Atlantic?"

Bob replied with a chuckle, "Sir, this is my very first trip on any boat that's not propelled by oars."

The Captain looked curiously at him. "Young fellow, I just don't believe you. You'd never be on your feet if this was your first trip."

Bob straightened up to his full height and replied, "Sir, if you've somehow managed to survive ten years of Depression farming in Saskatchewan, you can stand anything the North Atlantic has to offer. To tell the truth, sir, I'm in very high spirits. You see, this voyage is actually the first real holiday that I've ever had. I have a comfortable bed, a roof overhead, plenty of fresh air, no financial worries, and three square meals a day. What more could I want!"

Bob managed to survive several more trips on convoy duty before he was posted ashore. After the war, he moved to Vancouver

Island, was successful in business and finally settled down on a large waterfront property at Qualicum Beach. At eighty-three years of age he still keeps active renting cottages and RV campsites on his property.

He seldom thinks about the tough times in Saskatchewan over sixty years ago. He much prefers to focus on the future.

The School of Hard Knocks

When Charlie Stacey joined the army, his thirteen year old son Bill was given the responsibility of running the farm. For Bill it was a formidable challenge. Having just entered his teens, he did not have the strength or stamina that the job demanded. Moreover , he was small for his age, and could not even harness a horse without standing on a box. It was a major achievement for him to seed a crop on over two hundred acres. As the summer wore on, it became a crushing disappointment as yet another drought set in. The crop was so stunted and sparse that it was not worth harvesting.

That fall Bill also turned his back on farming. He decided to hunt for a job in Regina. He soon discovered that his inexperience and lack of education stood in his way. Consequently during his teens he moved frequently from one job to another. Eventually he found the right girl, got married and raised a family

Bill's departure as a teenager from a hard scrabble farm triggered a job search that lasted for many years, until eventually, as a senior citizen, he put down his roots on Vancouver Island. Here are some personal experience stories as told by Bill.

* * *

I left home when I was fourteen , with a grade six education. Any knowledge I acquired after this point in time was gained from "the school of hard knocks" - from many different job experiences. My objective was to find a job (almost any job would do) and become self-supporting and perhaps send some money home to help out the family. Usually when I landed a job it seemed that it either wouldn't suit me or I wouldn't suit the job for very long. This became most apparent to me during a short stay in Regina where in rapid succession I seemed to flit from one job to another. I got a job delivering ice for a few days for thirty-five cents an hour, then quit to become a grease monkey in a garage, then a busboy in a hotel. After just two days on that job I moved on to a bakery, then a brewery followed by a labouring job on a building mover's crew, and then on a construction job. My reasons for leaving some of these jobs might have been out of the ordinary, but at the time I thought they made good sense. For example: in the ice delivery business, when I accidentally dropped my watch between blocks of ice, the boss refused to allow me any time to retrieve it. As a grease monkey I was not paid for all the hours I worked, so I quit.

Then I got work in the bottling section of a brewery. I soon discovered that the other night shift employees were given six bottles of beer to take home after each completed work shift. But not me! I admit I was under legal drinking age, but when it came to beer I definitely had adult tastes. After receiving my first pay check I quit, and immediately got a job as a busboy in a hotel.

My sudden departure from the hotel was bizarre to say the least. On my first day of work the teenager operating the elevator took an immediate dislike to me. In my second day of employment, I used the elevator to bring a large tray of filled wine glasses from the kitchen to the convention floor. The elevator operator purposely stopped the cage about three inches below the floor level. As I exited the cage my foot caught the edge of the floor and I hurtled through the air landing headlong amongst the convention attendees amidst shattered glass and a flood of spilt wine.

My boss just happened to be in the vicinity, and when he saw the mess, he fired me on the spot. To add insult to injury, he demanded that I take off my busboy uniform then and there, which I did. I left the room and my job wearing only my underwear.

The very next day I got a job in a bakery, shaping loaves and feeding them into a gigantic oven. I intensely disliked working indoors in a hot environment, so I requested a job driving a bread delivery truck. When I was denied this opportunity, I again joined the unemployed.

In my next job I worked for a construction firm. I liked the work. I was outside in the fresh air, and it was summer time. However, I soon discovered that the owner of the company was very slow in paying wages . In the end I was paid only a fraction of my earnings. I quit with good reason, and was soon hired by a firm which moved buildings from place to place. I liked this job mainly because it was outdoors, and it was never boring. We were expected to do all kinds of work. However, the job was not without its hazards. On my last day of work, two of us were riding on top of the building as it was being moved along the highway. It was our job to lift the telephone wires and power lines as we passed under them.

By accident my fellow worker came in contact with a power line and suffered serious electrical burns. That night in bed I had a nightmare in which I was the victim of such an event. The next day I quit the job and sought greener pastures.

In 1952 I was hired to work on a seismic crew headquartered in Dawson Creek, and that's where I met Kay, my future wife. I was much too shy to come right out and ask her for a date. However, my buddy, a fellow worker, was courting Kay's girlfriend. I traipsed along to various social events, and was always paired up with Kay. A year later we were married. I still don't know how I got up enough nerve to propose to her.

Over the years I matured a lot, especially once we started to raise a family. I managed to hold onto a job for a longer period of time. Unfortunately, some of these jobs had serious safety limitations. Eventually, this danger caught up to me and I was seriously injured. At the time I had been working several years in a chemical plant in Edmonton. The product of this plant was Agent-Orange, a herbicide used by the Americans in the Viet Nam war. A primary part of the process involved large quantities of a mixture of sulphuric acid and alcohol shipped to our factory in forty-five gallon drums.

One particular barrel of this mixture apparently contained impurities which triggered an explosion. The contents were spewed over me, and I lost the sight of my left eye. Recent medical advances have renewed my hope of recovering my eyesight, although this accident occurred over thirty years ago.

Another hazardous job involved driving used cars from Toronto to be sold on the prairies. At the beginning this job looked attractive to me. A driver was supposed to be paid one cent per mile. He was expected to drive twelve hours a day. Living expenses en route were paid by the employer.

I nearly froze to death on my last trip. It was in early December. There were ten cars in our little caravan. Several newly-arrived English lads accompanied us as paying passengers. Occasionally they would drive for a few hours if a driver got over tired.

When we ended the day at Minot, North Dakota, the weather had turned cold and light snow was falling. It had been a long day so I went to bed right after supper. In those days I was a very sound sleeper and it took some time to get me out of bed in the morning. Unbeknownst to me, the other drivers had packed up early in the morning and left for Regina. What a shock for me when I finally got up! They had taken my suitcase. I had no money and no transportation.

I decided to hitchhike to Regina, which was around two hundred fifty miles north of Minot. I did not have a warm winter coat, just a light jacket. Without having any breakfast, I started thumbing on the highway. It was bitter cold and I had to keep walking to keep warm.

I had walked five miles before a vehicle stopped for me. By this time I was shivering uncontrollably and my ears, fingers and toes were starting to freeze. I was picked up by the driver of a big truck who made deliveries for a meat packing company. I hadn't eaten for nearly fifteen hours. Each time the truck stopped to make a delivery, I took the liberty of eating a few frozen wieners.

When the truck completed its delivery route, it returned to base and I found myself stranded at the Canadian-USA border. I went to a nearby cafe and by reversing the charges, I telephoned Grandmother Kellogg and told her of my plight. Several local men enjoying their coffee overheard my tale of woe. One of them, a local miner, approached me after the phone call. He was quite concerned about my circumstances and he decided to help me out. He took me home where I met his wife and seven children. After giving me a substantial meal they gave me the warmest bed in the house. The next morning he gave me five dollars to cover bus fare to Regina. A few months later I had saved some money and I returned the loan plus another ten dollars to show my appreciation. Eventually we became better acquainted and exchanged Christmas cards for over twenty-five years.

My varied experiences which extended over several decades finally paid off when I applied for the job of gatekeeper of a Qualicum waterfront property. When this job was advertised there were over one hundred applicants. Why was I selected? I think there were two main reasons. I had learned to get along with people, any kind of people. And I could repair anything involving electricity, plumbing, carpentry or decorating.

For me, this is the best job I've ever had. Clean, saltwater air! No pollution! No mosquitoes or flies! Peace and quiet! There is no age exclusion! If I live to be ninety, I'll still have this job. A free-rent waterfront home is my pay plus whatever incidental jobs I do for individual home owners. Kay and I love shellfish, and Manila clams and Japanese oysters are very prolific on "our beach".

Good-Bye Saskatchewan!

Graduating from high school should have been a very rewarding experience for me. There should have been a feeling of accomplishment and success, plus a great deal of satisfaction.

The year was 1942, and although I was more than pleased with passing Grade XII, I had some serious misgivings. I felt that my life had suddenly reached a state of crisis.

I had good reason to be concerned. There simply were no jobs in my home town of Cudworth, Saskatchewan. Surprisingly enough, there was practically no unemployment, either. Young people left town to further their education or to join the armed services. A few were able to find good-paying jobs in Ontario or in B.C., where there had been some degree of economic recovery soon after the war began.

I had just turned seventeen, and was still too young to join the military. I had vaguely thought of becoming a teacher. During war time, there was a shortage of teachers, and it was possible for a high school graduate to obtain a temporary teaching certificate with a minimum of training. Unfortunately, my father was not in a position to help me financially. He had already sold the family car to pay for my oldest sister's education in a business school.

I didn't know which way to turn. Fortunately, my uncle Laurie came to my rescue, and offered me temporary employment on his farm.

In 1938, Uncle Laurie had bought a farm near Lac Vert, about sixty miles east of Cudworth. Entering the farming business at that time was risky. Grain prices were still depressed. For many farmers, it was a hand-to-mouth existence. During the 1930's, Uncle Laurie had been a grain buyer in the Alberta Pacific elevator in Cudworth. When he bought the farm, he was successful in getting his job transferred to Lac Vert. He would continue to bring home a monthly pay cheque. He also made a partnership agreement with his younger brother Oscar who would take charge of farm operations. In exchange, Oscar would earn title to one hundred and sixty acres of farm land.

Oscar was a very practical and experienced farmer. He had a way with animals, and could ride a horse like a cowboy. He was a super mechanic, blacksmith and carpenter. The partnership between Laurie and Oscar became a success. Oscar tackled the practical problems on the farm. Uncle Laurie's steady income provided a good living for his family (wife and four children) as well as working capital to construct farm buildings and purchase farm machinery and equipment.

Starting in 1939, I spent my summer holidays on Uncle Laurie's farm. To earn my keep, I took on chore responsibilities. I helped Oscar with various farm projects such as grinding animal feed (chop), driving a tractor in summer fallowing, manuring the barn, and feeding and watering two hundred pigs.

My most outlandish job experience on the farm was riding a breaking plow. This piece of farm equipment was used to convert raw bush land into farm land. It was a very essential machine on Uncle Laurie's farm which was covered by a dense growth of white poplar. This bush land would have to be cleared and plowed before it could be cultivated.

During my first summer on the farm, about twenty-five acres of cleared land was scheduled to be plowed. To accomplish this task, Oscar drove a 15-30 McCormick Deering tractor which pulled the breaking plow. Because the soil was very productive, the trees were unusually large. Many of the stumps exceeded twelve inches in diameter. If the plow hit the centre of a big stump, the entire operation would come to a complete stop. Large stumps had a large root mass, and the roots would become entangled between the plow frame and the coulter (a vertical cutting bar in front of the plow share). When this space became completely plugged with roots, the plow would cease to function.

Oscar solved the problem by mounting an old tractor seat on the plow frame. It became my job to sit on this seat and prevent roots from jamming by using a hooked metal rod. At the best of times, it was a bumpy, uncomfortable ride. It was sometimes dangerous. when the plow hit a big, impenetrable stump, the entire unit would come to a sudden, jolting stop. If I didn't manage to grab onto the plow frame, I would be hurled through the air onto the plowed furrows behind the machine.

I particularly enjoyed the 1942 harvest, my last season on the farm. I was in good health and I was strong enough to do a man's job without becoming exhausted. The working day was long and tedious. The objective was to make maximum use of daylight hours so that the crop would be harvested as soon as possible. We woke up in the dark before 5 a.m.. We first fed, curried and harnessed the horses. Then we sat down to our breakfast under the dim light of a kerosene lamp. Our breakfast was more a feast that a simple meal. We were served bacon, sausages, potatoes, eggs, pork and beans, pancakes, toast, porridge and gallons of milk and coffee. We worked very hard and we needed to load up on calories. No one on a threshing crew ever gained weight!

Our field work began as the sun became visible. I would drive along the endless rows of stooks, stopping frequently to fork bundles of grain onto my hay rack. Once the rack was fully loaded, I drove to the threshing machine and rapidly fed the bundles into this noisy, hungry monster.

Around mid-morning, we were provided with a "snack" delivered to the threshing site. There would be two or three kinds of sandwiches, cookies, cake and pie plus cold milk. I was pleasantly surprised at my newly acquired appetite.

Our horses also worked very hard. By mid-day they needed food, water and a rest. The crew took advantage of this pause in the workday to rest and eat another meal.

Before entering the kitchen, we washed our hands and faces at a bench out in the yard. An ample amount of very warm water was provided. We were liberally coated with sweat-streaked dust. Upon finishing my ablutions, I discovered that only one towel had been provided for the entire crew (seven of us). After we all had cleaned up, the towel was a sodden grimy mess. This may sound unsanitary, but we managed to maintain good health for the entire harvest season.

On the whole, I enjoyed the company of my fellow crewmen. However, they seemed to enjoy playing tricks on me, probably because I was the youngest, and not really a farm boy. I remember on one occasion, someone removed the king pin from the double-tree on my wagon while I was unloading into the threshing machine. This meant that the horses were no longer attached to my wagon. When I finished unloading, I grabbed the reins and signalled my horses to go. The horses took off, but the wagon did not. I could hear the sound of the crew's laughter above the noise of the threshing machine.

When harvesting was completed, I stayed on at Uncle Laurie's farm, even though an extra hand was seldom needed.

On my very last job on the farm, Oscar and I hauled grain on sleds to Uncle Laurie's grain elevator in Lac Vert. It was bitter cold so we walked to keep warm, rather than riding on top of the loads. Despite wearing a pair of woollen mitts covered by leather mitts, my hands became very cold. I was soon convinced that my hands were freezing, and I told Oscar (who always had a practical solution to any problem). He stopped the horses and beckoned me to witness his procedure. He stood alongside the rear end of one of his horses, removed his mitts and trust his cold bare hand between the horse's hind legs, an area which, of course, was as warm as toast. I was certain that as Oscar's hand hit home, the horse flinched, rolled his eyes plaintively and shuddered. However, it did not become unsettled. From previous episodes, I had become convinced that Oscar could communicate with horses. So when he assured me that the horse did not mind the feel of an icy hand, I repeated the action with one of my horses. Circulation was soon restored, and we continued our journey to the grain elevator. Later in the day, I did notice a slight horse odour from my hands.

Finally, a week before Christmas, I returned to Cudworth.

As the new year dawned, I was living in my parents' home and was unemployed. I soon became frustrated, bored and anxious about my future. Finally, I got a job, if you could call it that. I earned fifty cents for splitting more that a cord of white poplar firewood. That worked out to six cents an hour. This sounds like a very meagre wage, but it was not out of line. For example, during harvesting, I was paid one dollar a day, for labouring very hard for at least ten hours.

I finally realized that I would have to leave my home town and seek my fortune elsewhere. I was aware that a couple of other high school graduates from Cudworth had found good jobs in Ontario. Was there a future for me in some other province?

I decided to travel to the government employment office in Saskatoon and make enquiries. During my interview, I expressed my willingness to work anywhere in Canada. I was told that I would be contacted if any out-of-province jobs materialized.

A week later, I was informed by telephone that sawmill jobs were available at Youbou on Vancouver Island. I was then told that the personnel manager from ITM (Industrial Timber Mills) would be in Saskatoon in two days to interview job candidates.

The personnel manager informed a group of us that because of the war, ITM was very short-handed, both in the sawmill at Youbou and in nearby logging camps. Sawmill jobs paid sixty-five cents an hour for day shift, and seventy cents an hour for night shift. But then he said, "This probably sounds like real good pay; however, you look strong enough to be loggers. You could get a logging job for eight-one cents an hour."

His comments almost floored me. I could not imagine having a job that paid over six dollars per day. I visualized that I would be rich in a few months. It is easy to dream when you are just seventeen years old.

It was good-bye Cudworth! Good-bye Saskatchewan! And hello to the forests of British Columbia, where I found opportunities which led me to a rewarding life-time career in forestry.

In the Good Old Days

My fourteen year-old grandson, Cameron, and I were sipping strawberry milkshakes at the Dairy Queen on our way home after his hockey game.

I always get a big kick out of watching his games. I especially enjoy when he sends a Gretzky-like pass to a winger in good scoring position. In my opinion, this reflects the real spirit of the game, rather than stick-handling the puck the length of the ice all by himself.

Cameron's game has sure improved this past year. Starting in April, he attended a hockey school every Saturday and Sunday until the end of July. The arena sessions were very thorough and demanding, and he enjoyed every minute. To really keep in good shape, the players completed a long cross-country run at the end of each Sunday session.

Watching Cameron play hockey takes me back sixty years or more, to a small Saskatchewan town where I learned the game. What a contrast to Cameron's situation! In Cudworth, Saskatchewan, we had an open-air rink, with natural ice. Extremely low temperatures would often open up long, deep, ankle-twisting cracks in the ice. Conditioning the ice sheet relied upon primitive methods. Instead of a Zamboni flooding several times a day, we were lucky to get a weekly flooding using a hand-held hose. Snow removal was a tedious and strenuous job, using hand-operated scrapers and scoop shovels.

I paused in my reverie to have another taste of my milkshake. Cameron immediately spoke up. "Excuse me, Grandpa, I want to ask you a question about the time when you were my age."

"Go right ahead, Cameron."

"You have already told me a bit about playing hockey in your teens. Sometimes you mention 'the good old days'. What I want to know is this. Outside of hockey, what was so good about your life as a teen-ager then?"

I guess Cameron could not visualize how a teenage boy could possibly enjoy Depression-era, small town, Saskatchewan. After all, we had no organized sports programs, no computers, no television, no electronic gadgets nor video games. I had already told him that we lacked a gymnasium in our school, and our town had no swimming pool or movie theatre.

So how did we have fun despite being deprived of so many diversions and amusements? The answer is very simple: we did not feel deprived! We simply didn't know any better. We always tried to make the best of the situation. As our parents had done before us, we took our enjoyment out of simple activities, many of them self-motivated.

Little did Cameron realize that we experienced many more important short comings in those days. For example, my father could not afford to drive his 1928 Chevrolet sedan during the Depression. This meant no summer vacation trips for our family. We had an ancient battery-operated radio but we could only afford to operate it during long winter nights. We had very few conveniences: no bathroom, no running water, no refrigerator or ice box, no powered washing machine. Not even an electric toaster. For heating and cooking we used mostly poplar fire wood, which was stacked in a huge wood box in the kitchen. During the winter it was my job to keep it full at all times.

Cameron interrupted my thoughts. "Grandpa, you also told me about terrible blizzards and forty-below weather. How could you possibly have fun outdoors?"

I let him know that severe blizzards were not common. During a bad one we spent little, if any, time outdoors. Sometime during a severe cold snap we were even allowed to stay home from school. I never objected to being kept in-doors because reading was my greatest passion. Sometimes the problem was finding something to read. There was no public library, and the school library had just a few books.

I then told Cameron that because our winters were cold, we simply learned to adapt, and take advantage of the cold weather. We dressed appropriately: fleece-lined long-johns, heavy wool socks, helmets with warm ear flaps, toques, sweaters, wind breakers, and wool mittens inside of leather mitts.

Hockey was our main outdoor pursuit. When ice was available, we played at the skating rink. If the rink was occupied by recreational skaters, we played our own particular brand of street hockey. We had no accessory hockey equipment. No helmets, gloves or pads. No uniforms. Our hockey team presented a confusing appearance with so many different coloured sweaters without identifying names or numbers. We had no regulation hockey pants. We all wore long pants tucked into heavy wool stockings.

For street hockey, we used frozen horse buns as pucks and usually a scoop shovel in lieu of a goalie stick. The supply of horse buns was bottomless. In those days horses provided the primary source of winter transportation. Few people operated cars. In any case, once the roads were plugged by snow drifts, there was no equipment or money available to clear the highways.

Cameron commented: "There's something else that I'd like you to tell me. When I watch the TV weather channel I sometimes hear warnings of extreme wind-chill. How did you cope with that? You must have had some awful high wind-chill numbers."

I explained to Cameron that this expression was unknown in our little town when I was young. If we had been familiar with "wind-chill", it probably would not have altered our attitude towards winter anyway. We sometimes experienced frost-bitten fingers or toes or ears, but we always had enough sense to come in from the cold before any serious damage developed.

Then I told him about other outdoor winter activities. On very rare occasions we were treated to an evening hay ride by an uncle who farmed near town. A balmy clear night was ideal: a million twinkling stars; northern lights dancing from horizon to horizon; the melodic jingle of tiny harness bells; the steam vapour rising from a perfectly matched team of spirited; high-stepping black horses.

And many songs and much laughter. We sang mostly popular songs plus some traditional Christmas carols and old songs that our parents had handed down. One of our favorites was "You are My Sunshine", and this would get sung several times during the ride. The sleigh was covered with a thick bed of straw. There may well have been some cuddling beneath the straw, but there was too much laughter and singing for any serious hanky-panky. The evening would end with a big mug of steaming cocoa and home-made cookies.

Cameron piped up again. "Tell me something, Grandpa. If the roads became impassable for vehicles during the winter, how would you get mail and shipments of food and stuff?"

I told him about our railway service. We got only four trains a week, since it was only a branch line. Two trains headed north to Prince Albert, and two headed south to Totzke. The train was powered by a huge coal-fired locomotive The most distinctive feature was the long-drawn-out whistle that could be heard from miles away. I can still hear this haunting sound if I close my eyes and dream a little. Since the railway was our life-line with civilization, it had to be cleared of snow by a huge snow plough.

The snow drifts produced by winter storms provided an additional recreational activity for me. Our front yard was enclosed by a picket fence, which generated the build-up of a deep snow drift only a few feet from the house. I would spend hours on my belly or in a crouched position digging tunnels and imagining that I was an Eskimo.

When I turned fifteen years of age, I was surprised by an extraordinary Christmas gift. My father had painstakingly made a pair of skis for me. These gave me the freedom to explore a large area south and west of Cudworth. This hilly country was covered by hundreds of acres of semi-open brush land used mostly for pasturage during the summer.

I set snares for rabbits which my mother converted into appetizing stews. I also trapped weasels and learned how to skin them and prepare their pelts for market. The best price I ever got was a dollar and twenty-five cents for a weasel skin twenty-four inches long from nose to the black tip of its tail. I often carried a small single-shot .22 rifle, and occasionally shot a prairie chicken or partridge for the table.

We had no school gym so at recess we had to be inventive. During spring thaw we would traipse out of the school yard to a nearby pond and scamper across the thin ice. The objective was to run across the pond without breaking through the ice. At a certain stage the ice would become flexible and a billowing effect like a wave occurred as we ran across. We called it "rubber ice". Most of us seemed to be invincible, but eventually someone would break through and get dunked in three to four feet of water. At that point, the law would be laid down by the principal and we would be forbidden to leave the school yard during recess.

As snow melt continued, patches of bare ground would be exposed. The girls played hopscotch or skipped rope, while the boys got reacquainted with marble games. This "sport" created secondary scam activities, which involved gambling for marbles. These scams included dropping a marble about three feet with the intention of hitting a hole in a small box on the floor. In order to play you paid one marble. If you succeeded in hitting the hole you would win five marbles. The hole was small and there were few winners.

Another scam involved a punch board. We would get a used one from the cafe, and insert bits of rolled paper in each hole. A fee of one marble was charged for one punch paper. Most of the papers paid zero.

Our principal caught wind of these gambling activities. He lectured us about developing principles of honesty and fair play. The gambling would be immediately curtailed but would certainly reappear the next spring.

Also in the spring, one of our more physically demanding activities revolved around pest control. I would walk about a mile to my uncle Joe's farm where my male cousins and I would observe the movements of the local gopher populations. We would select a particular gopher hole which was occupied and which was near water. My smallest cousin, not yet strong enough to carry a five-gallon bucket of water, was assigned the job of lookout in case gophers would try to escape while we were refilling our water buckets. He would kneel on the ground, straddling the gopher hole, ready to pounce on any gopher that surfaced. The rest of us filled buckets at a nearby pond and carried them to the hole. We poured the water into the hole, forcing the gophers to come to the surface. They usually had families in early spring, so from one hole we often obtained half a dozen critters as they surfaced. We were paid a penny per gopher tail as this little animal was regarded as a serious grain-consuming pest.

Most of the mosquito-breeding ponds that we used for a water supply dried up as the season progressed, so we changed our pest control tactics. We made a small noose out of binder twine and placed it carefully around an occupied gopher hole. The tail end of the twine was laid out in a straight line about ten feet from the hole. Then we stretched out on the ground, belly down, and watched the hole for any action. When a gopher's head suddenly appeared, we yanked hard on the twine and usually throttled a gopher. These savage practices of sixty years ago would certainly not sit well with today's S.P.C.A.

Summer temperatures allowed greater freedom and flexibility out-doors. We played baseball or soft ball at school during our lunch break. With no interference or coaching by adults both boys and girls had a great time. We usually had only one ball, so a game was often interrupted while we searched the bushes for the ball.

Our baseball field could not compare with the well-manicured field at Cameron's school. The infield at my school was gravelly, and sliding into base was a no-no. The outfield was riddled with gopher holes, and a fielder had to keep one eye on the ball and the other on the ground to avoid a sprained ankle.

Playing cowboys and outlaws was also popular during summer holidays. We made wooden rifles and pistols which discharged rubber bands made from discarded inner tubes from a local garage. The pistols were equipped with clothes pins to hold the stretched rubber bands. For the rifles, we used two intricate levers for a triggering device.

Another game designed for summer days was "playing knife". This involved a set sequence of pocket knife maneuvers - each with a distinct title. One worked up gradually, completing each step in the sequence. If your knife failed to stick in the ground, you lost your turn, and your opponent took over. I've long since forgotten the name of each step. I do remember that "jumping the river" was the final step. To complete the game the blade was stuck into the ground at an angle. You then hit the handle with the side of your hand, sending the knife twirling through the air. If on landing, the blade stuck into the ground, you were a winner.

During the summer our town would be blessed with a movie every two weeks (if we were lucky). The projectionist (usually from out of town) would set up his equipment in the town hall.

Viewing was not that great since the floor did not slope. Unpadded benches were very uncomfortable. The price of admission was fifteen cents for high school students; however, there was a limited opportunity to earn a free ticket if you were hired to perform an advertising job. Usually three teenagers took on the job as town criers. On show night around supper time they would parade along every street in town. Every few minutes they would ring a bell to attract attention and they would yell in their most melodious voices:

Show tonight
At the town hall
Starts at 8:30 p.m.
A good comedy
And an excellent feature.

On warm summer evenings after dark we played games on vacant property beneath a street light. The most popular games were Hide and Seek, Run Sheep Run, Simon says, and 1-2-3 Red Light.

I could see that Cameron had had enough of my reminiscing He was getting fidgety. In fact, he was making quite audible slurping noises while toying with the dregs of his milkshake. I had become completely absorbed in nostalgia, and could probably have kept on talking for ages.

It was time to end this visit. Cameron put the cap on it.

"Grandpa, we've finished our milkshakes and I'm supposed to go home and do my homework." And then he added: "I certainly enjoyed you stories. They sounded like a lot of fun - but I think I'll stick to becoming a great hockey player."

No Fixed Address

At eighty-five years of age, John Striha is a very highly regarded senior citizen of Victoria. His presence exudes an air of maturity, respectability and public spiritedness. After thirty active years of promoting and improving extended health care, and serving as Board Chairman of the Juan de Fuca Hospital Society, he still devotes a generous amount of time, energy, and money to these causes.

If you closely observed John these days, you would never in your wildest dreams speculate that here is a man who, over sixty years ago, was a hobo riding freight trains for free while job-seeking in western Canada.

John's father was a Russian who left the Ukraine in 1905 and emigrated to Chicago. In 1912 he left the USA and homesteaded near Viceroy, about fifty miles south of Moose Jaw.

John was born on this farm in 1919. He completed his elementary education in a nearby one-room country school which covered Grades I to VIII. He then had to look elsewhere to continue his education. The nearest high school was in Viceroy, too distant to commute from the farm. Instead, an arrangement was made for him to live in a Viceroy boarding house which catered to five or six school teachers. There he obtained room and board in exchange for doing household chores. His main responsibilities were peeling potatoes, washing dishes, filling the firewood box and carrying buckets of water from a well to the kitchen and bathroom.

In 1934, southern Saskatchewan experienced a very severe drought. On the Striha farm the crop yields were too low to even justify harvesting costs. John heard that a group of young men was planning to travel in the box of a two-ton truck in search of harvesting jobs. He decided to join them. He was in desperate need of money for clothes and school supplies, and his family would not be able to help him because of the total crop failure. He believed that he was strong enough to do a man's job, although he was still a few weeks short of his fourteenth birthday.

The crew of harvesters traveled north and soon found jobs west of Battleford. Although John was eager and willing, he soon discovered that pitching bundles on a threshing crew was punishing work for a fourteen year old. By mid-afternoon his strength would begin to fade. Fortunately, his boss thought well of him, and toward the end of the day he would unload John's hayrack to give him a rest. Somehow, John managed to survive nearly a month on the threshing crew, and returned home with nearly all of his earnings.

John completed high school in 1937 and again worked on a harvesting job that fall. He knew that he could not find a local job during the winter, so he decided to seek work in B.C. After a little practice, he became a successful hitch hiker and managed to reach Vancouver in record time.

Vancouver turned out to be a big disappointment. Each day he walked the streets for many hours seeking any type of work without any success. He soon began to understand the magnitude of the unemployment problem. He was not the only stubble-jumper who had traveled west with hopes. After three weeks of frustration, he hitch-hiked to the Okanagan to live with family friends until the spring of 1938. He then returned home, helped with the harvest and with farm chores until the spring of 1939.

The idea of becoming a genuine hobo riding from place to place on freight trains began to take shape. There were compelling reasons. He visualized a carefree life with the lure of adventure. He would meet new faces and discover new places, and he just might stumble onto a decent job. One thing for sure, traveling around the country would certainly take him away from the drudgery of farm chores. A steady routine of manuring barns, milking cows and taking care of many farm animals no longer presented much appeal for him.

Before boarding a west-bound train in Moose Jaw, John first visited a pool hall. There he met several young men his age who had been drifting from place to place looking for work. They advised him to avoid the Moose Jaw railway yards which were patrolled by railway cops. Instead, they suggested that he could "hop a freight" along a stretch of track west of town where an adverse grade slowed the train to a crawl. By following their advice, John easily boarded a train and his life as a hobo began to unfold.

The first day the train took him to Medicine Hat, and he disembarked as it slowed down on the outskirts of the city. John soon discovered that local jobs were non-existent. He also heard that job prospects were supposed to be much better in B.C. Again, he headed west on a freight train, stopping briefly at Trail and then traveling on to Kimberley.

Kimberley seemed to be a popular place for hobos, mainly because it could boast of a first class "hobo jungle", in other words, an attractive camping ground for bums. This "home away from home" was located near the railway tracks in a widely-spaced grove of trees with a panoramic view of the mountains across the valley. A big pile of discarded railway ties provided plenty of dry wood for camp fires and there were trout in a nearby stream.

When John arrived, he discovered that there were already more than twenty hobos in the jungle. Some were still in their teens, most were in their twenties and there were a few grizzled veterans nearing middle age. On the whole, they proved to be a friendly bunch. In the evening, several mouth organs appeared and John fell asleep as the haunting music sifted through the trees. His new life as a hobo certainly had some enjoyable moments.

During his stay at Kimberley, John learned to improve his technique in the art of scrounging for meals. He confined his efforts to a subdivision owned by the mining company and occupied by its employees who had steady jobs and could afford to give hand outs to hobos. He also learned to always offer to split wood, weed gardens or do any chores before asking for food. He learned the importance of keeping his clothes clean and to always wear a smile when the householder opened the door. John promised himself that when his hobo days were over, he would write an essay on how to become an efficient pan handler and scrounger.

Although John enjoyed the companionship in the Kimberley jungle, he decided to move on. He had found no work, and it was becoming more difficult to barter work for a home-cooked meal. One newly acquired technique of obtaining food was to visit a butcher shop just before closing time. In those days, limited refrigeration facilities did not allow keeping cut-up meat for long. John would ask the butcher if he had any stew meat left over from the day's display case. Usually, the butcher would donate some. Occasionally, John would pay a token five cents a pound.

He would share his booty with several other hobos and make a big pot-luck stew. Fresh vegetables, probably filched from someone's garden, would go into the pot. Donated day-old bread would add variety.

John left Kimberley on a freight train and arrived at Penticton the same day. He was amazed at both the size and convenience of the Penticton hobo jungle. Indigents by the score arrived from across Canada in the hope of getting hired to pick fruit. The attraction was so great that when John arrived, he discovered that there were already five hundred hobos camped in this jungle. The camp was large, clean and well controlled by twice-daily visits by the Provincial police.

It was still too early in the summer for fruit picking in the Okanagan valley so John hopped a freight and headed south. He stopped briefly in Summerland, where the hobo jungle was located in a junk yard littered with old cars. Previous hobos had constructed fairly comfortable shelters by using old car bodies, the roofs to keep out the rain, the upholstered seats for comfortable beds.

John got his first real job at Osoyoos where he picked tomatoes for two weeks during very hot weather. Daily maximum temperatures exceeded one hundred degrees Fahrenheit. Apparently, the tomatoes would lose quality if picked during the heat of the day. Consequently, picking took place on a split-shift basis: from 4:00 a.m. to 9:00 a.m. and again from 6:00 p.m. to 9:00 p.m. The pay rate, thirty-five cents per hour, was very generous, certainly more than John had ever earned on threshing crews in Saskatchewan.

When the tomato crop had been completely picked, John got hired to pick apricots. When this job ended, he headed north to Salmo where he was offered four dollars a day to work as a mucker in a gold mine. The thought of working underground did not appeal to John; however, the owner promised to promote him to the first surface job that became open. Unfortunately, before John's first pay day came due, the mine went bankrupt and John left without getting paid.

At the pool hall in Salmo, John heard that one could earn good money fighting forest fires. He decided to team up with three other hobos and hang out at the Ranger station in case a fire fighting job materialized. On the very next day a lightening storm occurred, and started over a dozen fires in the Ranger district. John's little crew was immediately hired and sent out to fire camp. The food was substantial but not fancy. The hourly pay was very low; however, the time keeper was very generous and massive amounts of over time were accumulated.

The job was ended by a heavy rain, and John received a cheque for over forty dollars. He decided to look for a job in Alberta.

He caught a freight to High River and was soon hired to work in a dairy. He stayed there until the spring of 1940 and then decided to join the R.C.A.F. His goal was to become a pilot; however, his eyesight was not acceptable. Since coming to Alberta, John had been taking a correspondence course to learn shorthand and typing. With these credentials he was hired by the CPR in Calgary as an assistant secretary to the superintendent. After five months on the job, he again tried to join the R.C.A.F., this time as an office worker. He was successful and became an administrative clerk.

John served several years in England where he met Pamela who became his wife. Upon his return to Canada in 1945, he served briefly in Vancouver and in Victoria before he was discharged. He and Pam had fallen in love with Victoria and they decided to put down permanent roots in that city. For John, this decision signified the end to almost ten years of a nomadic life style: first as a hobo, and then in the R.C.A.F.

On looking back over his hobo days, John realized that he had been helped through tough times by many kind-hearted people. He decided to give something back to society in return. He first became involved in community affairs by becoming active in the School Board. Gradually, he broadened his scope until he took on a leading role in the health care system for senior citizens.

Although John has been a senior citizen for some years, he has not slowed down appreciably. He still experiences a strong urge to travel, which he attributes to his hobo days so very long ago. Fortunately, he can well afford the luxury of traveling in comfort in a motor home instead of on top of a box car.